Addie
on the Inside

Other Books by James Howe

Novels
A Night Without Stars
Morgan's Zoo
The Watcher
The Misfits
Totally Joe

Edited by James Howe
The Color of Absence: Twelve Stories About Loss and Hope
*13: Thirteen Stories That Capture the Agony and Ecstasy
  of Being Thirteen*

Sebastian Barth Mysteries
What Eric Knew
Stage Fright
Eat Your Poison, Dear
Dew Drop Dead

Bunnicula Books
Bunnicula (with Deborah Howe)
Howliday Inn
The Celery Stalks at Midnight
Nighty-Nightmare
Return to Howliday Inn
Bunnicula Strikes Again!
Bunnicula Meets Edgar Allan Crow

Tales from the House of Bunnicula
It Came from Beneath the Bed!
Invasion of the Mind Swappers from Asteroid 6!
Howie Monroe and the Doghouse of Doom
Screaming Mummies of the Pharaoh's Tomb II
Bud Barkin, Private Eye
The ~~Amazing~~ Odorous Adventures of Stinky Dog

Bunnicula and Friends

The Vampire Bunny
Hot Fudge
Rabbit-cadabra!
Scared Silly
Creepy-Crawly Birthday
The Fright Before Christmas

Pinky and Rex Series

Pinky and Rex
Pinky and Rex Get Married
Pinky and Rex and the Mean Old Witch
Pinky and Rex and the Spelling Bee
Pinky and Rex Go to Camp
Pinky and Rex and the New Baby
Pinky and Rex and the Double-Dad Weekend
Pinky and Rex and the Bully
Pinky and Rex and the New Neighbors
Pinky and Rex and the Perfect Pumpkin
Pinky and Rex and the School Play
Pinky and Rex and the Just-Right Pet

Picture Books

There's a Monster Under My Bed
There's a Dragon in My Sleeping Bag
Teddy Bear's Scrapbook (with Deborah Howe)
Horace and Morris but mostly Dolores
Horace and Morris Join the Chorus (but what about Dolores?)
Kaddish for Grandpa in Jesus' name amen
Horace and Morris Say Cheese (which makes Dolores sneeze!)

Addie
on the Inside

JAMES HOWE

ATHENEUM BOOKS FOR YOUNG READERS   New York   London   Toronto   Sydney

ATHENEUM BOOKS FOR YOUNG READERS
An imprint of Simon & Schuster Children's Publishing Division
1230 Avenue of the Americas, New York, New York 10020
ATHENEUM BOOKS FOR YOUNG READERS is a registered trademark of Simon & Schuster, Inc.
For information about special discounts for bulk purchases, please contact
Simon & Schuster Special Sales at 1-866-506-1949 or business@simonandschuster.com.
The Simon & Schuster Speakers Bureau can bring authors to your live event.
For more information or to book an event, contact the Simon & Schuster Speakers
Bureau at 1-866-248-3049 or visit our website at www.simonspeakers.com.
The text for this book is set in Gotham.
Manufactured in the United States of America

2 4 6 8 10 9 7 5 3
Library of Congress Cataloging-in-Publication Data
Howe, James, 1946–
Addie on the inside / James Howe.
p. cm.
Summary: Outspoken thirteen-year-old Addie Carle learns about love,
loss, and staying true to herself as she navigates seventh grade, enjoys
a visit from her grandmother, fights with her boyfriend, and endures
gossip and meanness from her former best friend.
ISBN 978-1-4169-1384-9 (hardcover)
[1. Novels in verse. 2. Identity—Fiction. 3. Self-acceptance—Fiction.
4. Grandmothers—Fiction. 5. Schools—Fiction.
6. Interpersonal relations—Fiction.]
I. Title.
PZ7.5.H69Ad 2011
[Fic]—dc22   2010024497
0911 FFG

To Zoey

Prologue

Who Do You See?

The poems that follow
are written in the voice of
Addie on the inside.

But this poem is written
from me to you,
writer to reader.

I want to ask you:
Who do you see
when you think of me?

Am I young or old,
wise or a fool,
teacher or friend?

Who do you see
when you think of you?
Are you an outsider,

cool, distant, angry,
swimming against the current,
or are you in the flow?

When they tell you,
This is who you are,
do you say yes or no?

Who do you see
when you look at them?
You know the ones I mean:

the others, the olders,
the youngers, the ones
who are not you, not

like you or your friends,
who wear the labels
you give them until

they give them back,
saying, *I believe these
belong to you.*

Who do you see when a girl
like Addie walks down the hall,
sharp-eyed, tall,

when a girl like Addie
raises her hand in class
for the hundredth time

offering opinion as fact
and outrage as opinion,
wearing her attitudes

more comfortably than her
less than awesome clothes?
Who do you see

when you look beyond
the skin and the surface,
when you drift to sleep,

when you are the person
no one else knows? Who
are you on the inside?

Don't answer these questions.
Not yet. First, open your eyes,
your mind, your heart.

See.

—James Howe

Addie
on the Inside

This Purgatory of
the Middle School Years

You Are Who They Say You Are

They say in the seventh grade
you are who they say you are,
but how can that be true?

How can I be a
Godzilla-girl
lezzie loser
know-it-all
big mouth
beanpole
string bean
freaky tall
fall-down
spaz attack
brainiac
maniac
hopeless nerd
bad word
brown-nosing
teacher's pet
showing off
just to get
attention—
oh,
and did I
mention:

flat-chested
(that's true)
badly dressed
(says you)
social climber
(such a lie)
rabble-rouser
(well, I try)
tree-hugging
tofu-eating
button-wearing
sign-waving
slogan-shouting
protest-marching
troublemaking
hippie-dippy
throwback
to another
time and place?

How can I be all that?
It's too many things to be.
How can I be all that and
still be true to the real me
while everyone is saying:

This
is
who
you
are.

Every morning I wake up worrying

and *not* about crushes
or acne or whether
I should stuff my bra
so people will know
I'm wearing one.

I worry about
global warming and
polar bears dying and
war and
more and
more and
more.

I worry about
injustice and
how to make the world
a better place,
because I contend
that if you are not part
of the solution,
you are part
of the problem.
I worry about
the rights of minorities
and I worry about
all the people

who love people
that the people who hate them
don't want them to love.

I worry about
my parents and
I worry about
my friends and
I worry about
people I don't even know
who have lost their homes
and their jobs and have
nowhere to go and
I worry about
what happens to
all of their pets and
I worry about
the economy and
the national debt.

I worry about
the animals that are
going extinct
and the animals that are
abused just so we can have
a new scent of perfume
or a new kind of shoes.

I worry how in the world
the world will ever be okay. Then
I turn off my alarm
and get on with the day.

Rush Hour

Morning. Toast. Butter. Jam.
Eggs? No thanks. I am
gathering up my homework,
they are blowing on their tea.

Grandma's coming for a visit.
That's nice, I say. Is it
for a weekend or a week?
Backpack. Keys. Other shoe.

A week or maybe more. Dad
shakes his head at bad
news in the paper. Cereal?
Only if there's Special K.

Why did I wear black pants?
Mom asks after a chance
encounter between both her legs
and both the cats.

Look at the time. Dishes. Sink.
Feed the cats. Quickly drink
the last of the orange juice.
Grab a sweater.

Joe's at the door. Let's go,
he calls out, and I know
I'm forgetting something.
Where's my kiss? calls Dad.

Peck on the cheek. Money
for lunch. Mom says, Honey,
remember what we talked about.
I've no idea what she means.

I will, I say, and I'm out the door,
the cats pushing ahead, off to explore.
Joe says something that
makes me laugh.

Sidewalks. Curbs. Friends wave
at us from the next street. They've
got backpacks. Toast. Butter. Jam.
Who knows why I'm happy.
I just am.

Becca Has Something to Say

My best friends are
Joe
and
Bobby
and
Skeezie,
and even though I have other friends,
these three are my best, oldest, truest,
and forever ones.

This morning, between English and art,
in the three minutes when the hall
is like a race being run by animals
sprung from their cages, when it's all
you can do to get to your locker
and get to your class,
Becca Wrightsman takes the time
to point out that my best friends are
all boys. "Really, Addie," she says,
"that's *so* gay." She smiles
as if *she* were my best and oldest
and truest and forever friend
before shouting, "Tonni, wait up!"

I stand there as she and Tonni
knock their heads together, laughing,
stand there as the other kids stampede by,
roar past, as bells ring and doors slam shut
up and down the hall,
stand there until I am the only one,
saying to no one at all:

"It is not."

"That's so gay"

is an expression I hate.
Do you mind if I change it
to "that's so straight"?

The Good Samaritan

Becca Wrightsman says to me—
out of nowhere at all—says to me,
"I can fix your look." This
is in the hall just before French.

Excuse me?

"Really, Addie." Twirling her
hair. "You need a makeover.
For starters you should wear a
bra." Dropping her voice,
raising her eyebrows. "Even if,
you know, there's nothing
there."

Excuse me?

"And you could use some
blush and then there's your
hair, that's going to be a
challenge. But you know me,
I love a challenge. Oops,
there's the bell. Gotta run.
TTFN."

Excuse me:

I do not know you
and I am wearing a bra
and nobody says TTFN
and now

  I am late

    for French.

Who is Becca Wrightsman

with her skintight jeans
and her pouty-pouty lips
and the way she moves her hips
that made Jimmy Lemon
collide with Jason Kline so
they both dropped their backpacks
at the very same time?
(I am so not kidding.)
With her perfect little purse
and her perfect phony tan
and the way she waves her hands
as if her nails are drying
and bats her doe-y eyes like
she's on the verge of crying.
(Give me a break.)
With her text message life
and her gossip girl demeanor
and the way there is nothing
she allows to come between her
and anything she wants.
With her taunts and her sneers
and all the little cruelties
she sprinkles through the day.
Where is she hiding *Miss Mary*
Mack, Mack, Mack, all dressed in
black, black, black, the hand-
smacking, Double-Dutching,

one-foot-hopping, bubble-popping girl
who saved her mother's back
by never stepping on a crack?
What ever happened
to the girl she used to be?
The girl who was friendly
to other girls, like me.

Now That She's Back

She was just a girl I played with sometimes.
I never even said goodbye. I never thought about her
in all the years she lived somewhere else. Now
that she's moved back, she never lets me forget.

Because I'm with DuShawn

Because I have a boyfriend,
because the boyfriend is DuShawn,
because DuShawn is popular,
I thought things would be different.
I thought everyone would say,
"Look at Addie. She's with DuShawn."
Instead, everyone says,
"Look at DuShawn.
What is *he* doing with *her*?"

The Mysterious Order
of the Lunchtime Table

Zachary sits quietly, sipping through a straw.
Kelsey averts her eyes from Bobby's, while
under the table their feet meet like old friends.
Joe and I do most of the talking. Skeezie and
DuShawn make most of the jokes. Hotheaded
Tonni gets angry for nothing as Royal nods
and says through a mouthful of Yoplait, "Uh-
huh, girl, tell it, uh-huh." Some days Amy
and Evie squeeze in, taking up space for one,
giggling softly at secrets they have earlier
whispered in each other's ears.

Becca isn't here, of course—too above it all
to care. And Tonni and Royal? They're here
only because DuShawn is here. And DuShawn?
He is here only because of me.

So it goes each day from 11:52 to 12:12.
The mysterious order of our lunchtime table,
when for a brief moment the Popular deign to
sit with the Un. O let us give thanks. Twenty
minutes of pretending that We Are All One.

An Unfortunate Conversation

"That girl has bazoobies bigger than my head,"
Royal says as Skeezie spits milk all over his tray
and half of the table. "And you got one *big*
head," says Tonni, whose full name is

"Tondayala Cherise DuPré! What are you
sayin', girl?" "I'm saying you got a big head
is all. Doesn't she got a big head, DuShawn?"
DuShawn flashes me a *help-me-out-here* look,
but I know when to keep my mouth
shut.

"It is true," Joe chimes in, "that Becca's bosoms
are bodacious." "Excellent use of alliteration,"
I say because I can't help myself, and now
everyone is staring at me and I feel my chest
growing flatter, which is a near mathematical
impossibility. Earlier I'd told Joe what Becca
had said to me about my needing a bra.
As if reading my mind, Joe says (not reading
the part of my mind that is screaming,
SHUT UP, JOE!), "Androgyny is cool, Addie.
Seriously, girls who look like boys are hot."
"You're gay," I say. "To you, anything
that looks like a boy is hot." Milk
is drying in dribbles on Skeezie's chin. His grin
grows so wide I can see every bit of food stuck

between his teeth and I find myself picturing
the teeth I can't see and imagining what is hidden
in the recesses there. I want to say to Skeezie,
"Close your lips," if only to divert attention away from me,
but it is too late. "Don't worry, Addie," says Tonni,
her eyes as friendly as the first frost, "you're just a little
behind the curve." "So to speak," says Skeezie,
which gets some laughter. Now I say it: "Skeezie,
close your lips." And this gets even more.

I cannot bring myself to look at DuShawn. I try hard
not to think the thought I have thought a million times
since we started going out, but I can feel it rising up
as the laughter is dying down: *What is he doing with me*
when he could be with a girl like Becca or Tonni?
Tonni says, "Addie is blessed with brains over boobs,"
and I resist the temptation
to praise the alliteration
and instead pray for release
from this purgatory of
the middle school years
when so many things
that never mattered before
and will never matter again

matter.

Tondayala Cherise DuPré

may have a name like a
puffed pastry

but she has eyes that say,
"I'm the hammer

and you're the nail."

I Wonder If She's Jealous

The way she says his name like
it's their little secret. The way
her hammer eyes watch me like
I'm a mystery she can't solve.
Me,
this plain-Jane white girl,
walking through the halls hand
in hand with the boy I think
she'd like for herself, black like her,
popular.

Is it possible? Could I be a girl
who makes other girls
jealous?

Well, if
that's the case,
I might just grow
to like it.

Skin

DuShawn once told me I have skin
the color of the inside of almonds,
then changed it to
peach
ice
cream.

DuShawn has skin the color
of a moonless night.

Holding hands,
folding black on white,
white on black,
we don't feel the color.

We feel the skin.

The Way It Happened

"So you want to go to the dance with me?"
back in September DuShawn boldly asked.
I was so clueless I had no idea he liked me.
So what if Skeezie had insisted DuShawn's
poking me all through pre-Columbian America,
spitballing me in the hall, and slipping that
whoopee cushion under me in homeroom
were clear declarations of love. How very
poetic. How very "How do I love thee?
Let me count the ways."
1. Poke
2. Spit
3. Fart
How very seventh-grade boy, and, really,
how is a girl supposed to know? But then
when he said, "So you want to go to the dance
with me?" and looked at me with guileless eyes,
well, I was surprised but not unpleasantly so.
"I would love to go to the dance with you,"
I told him. And he said, "Okay, then." And
I said, "Okay." And that's the way
it happened.

These Lips

I'm not a girl who kisses
or would ever be kissed
or so I thought. I mean,
look at me. These lips
are made for talking.

But one time DuShawn
said, "Shut up for once,
Addie." And he leaned
in and before I could say
"What are you doing?"

he did it.

Now I'm a girl who kisses
and secretly wishes
for more. These lips
keep talking but they get
lonelier than before.

Caught in the Act

"It is not like you to be staring out the window,
Addie Carle. It is not like you not to hear.
Come here, Addie, come to the board and solve
this equation."
                    I look at her with thinly
veiled contempt. *Ms. Wyman*, I want
to say as I make my way to the board,
have your lips never been kissed?
The thought of it almost makes me laugh,
almost until I remember that I am more
than a girl who has been kissed and stares
off into space remembering it. I am a girl
with a memory for numbers and a hunger
for words, a girl whose brain once mattered
more than her lips.
                    I slip past Ms. Wyman,
ashamed to have been caught in the act
of being normal.

I pick up the chalk.

          "Love makes fools
of us all," somebody once said. I set to work
on the numbers on the board, wishing
I could disprove the words in my head.

Ms. Wyman Never Answers My Questions

The other morning in homeroom I asked Ms. Wyman,
"Do you believe in God?" She gave me an odd look,
then looked away as if she hadn't heard or at best
thought my question absurd, so I asked it again:
"Ms. Wyman, do you believe in—"

                                        "I heard you
the first time, Addie, and your question has no
place in school." "Exactly my point," I replied
as she brushed me aside with a sigh and "Please rise
for the pledge." I waited, then asked, "If my question
has no place in school, then why do we say 'under
God' in the pledge?" Her voice had an edge as she
glared and said, "Addie, you do try my patience."

Unsolvable Equation

"Ms. Wyman hates me,"
I told my mother when I got
home from school that day.
We were lifting bags of
groceries from the trunk
of the Volvo. "It's because
I question her authority,
even though I don't really.
I just stick up for myself.
For heaven's sake, it was *only*
a question about God."
My mother pointed to one
of the many bumper stickers
on the back of our car.
"'**LORD, HELP ME BE THE PERSON**
MY CAT THINKS I AM'?" I read,
perplexed. "The one above it,"
my mother replied. "'**WELL-BEHAVED**
WOMEN SELDOM MAKE HISTORY.'
That is why she hates you,"
she said, grabbing for the jar
of pickles about to topple
from the top of the overstuffed
bag dangling from her left
arm. "I don't want to make
history. I just want to get
through homeroom and do well

in math," I answered, even though
I secretly do want to make
history.
          Just then the over-
stuffed bag ripped open
and the jar of pickles
crashed to the floor
of the porch, exploding
on contact. The cats went
ballistic. "Lousy plastic,"
my mother growled.
"That's it! From now on
we're bringing our own
bags. And they're going
to be hemp!" The only
thing that surprised me
about this statement was
that it had taken so long.
The bumper sticker above
WELL-BEHAVED WOMEN reads,
LESS PLASTIC IS FANTASTIC.

          We have since
switched to hemp so at least
one problem has been solved.
I am still, however, working
on the solution to this
equation:

If Addie = Smart Student,
and Ms. Wyman = Teacher Who
Likes Smart Students,
why does Ms. Wyman
hate Addie?

But Then There's Ms. Watkins

If I must suffer Ms. Wyman's ways
all through period seven,
at least Ms. Watkins in period eight
provides a bit of heaven.

She has this halo of frizzy hair
and wears these retro glasses.
(Not that it matters what she wears,
I'm talking about her classes.)

She tells us teaching is her life.
I've never seen such passion.
O how I love her fire, her mind,
her awesome sense of fashion.

(Not that I notice what she wears,
it's hardly worth the mention;
it's social studies taught with flair
that rivets my attention.)

Ms. Watkins actually *likes* the fact
that I'm smart and so outspoken.
She doesn't think it's all an act
or treat me like I'm broken.

"Well done, Addie!" she says with a smile
when I offer an observation
or a clever rebuttal or fresh insight
on a stale interpretation.

She said it today when I pointed out
how women are often cheated
of their rightful place in history books, how
their names are simply deleted.

Some boys laughed, and some girls, too,
one even called me mental.
But Ms. Watkins told me, "Good for you,"
and the rest was inconsequential.

After class she pulled me aside
to ask how my project was going.
Maybe it was just the light from behind
but I swear her hair was glowing.

"I *love* your hair," I blurted out.
I didn't mean to flatter.
I couldn't believe I'd said it aloud;
I mean, looks don't really matter.

Or maybe they do, I'm no longer clear.
I just know I've reasons myriad
to think Ms. Watkins the best teacher here
and to be grateful for eighth period.

The Real Reason People Think I'm Weird

It's not because I'm tall
or skinny as a board.
It's not my hair as limp
as seaweed washed ashore.

It's not even that I'm bright,
though that provides a clue,
or that I talk too much,
using words like *hitherto.*

It's mostly that I've broken
an unspoken rule.
I even dare to say it:
I love school.

NO ONE IS FREE WHEN OTHERS ARE OPPRESSED

(A Button on My Backpack)

Do you believe it to be true?
I do.
No one is free when others are oppressed.
So this spring I addressed it by starting a GSA.
Translation:
An alliance for the straight and the gay.

I did it for Joe, who is out, and for Colin,
who is not, and for all those who haven't got
the same rights as you and I
(if you and I happen to be straight).

But wait.
Here's what happened after school today:

We were having a meeting,
there were six of us there
(including Joe but not Colin,
who doesn't dare),
when some boys ran past the room
and banged on the door, shouting:

LEZZIES! FAGGOTS! FREAKS!

Mr. Daly rushed to see who it was
but they were too fast, they were gone.

"What makes them think," he said,
his voice shaking, his face burning red,
"what makes them think,
whoever they were at the door,
that they are more than anyone else,
that they are not different
in some way, too?"

Mr. Daly is my hero for agreeing to be
the faculty advisor for the GSA. Some say
it's because he has a son who's gay, but
I say it's because it's who he is.
"To thine own self be true," his favorite quote,
were the words he wrote on the board
the first day of English class last fall. Mr. D
helps us all see through the words we read
to the people we are.

He is full of quotes. He wrote this one
on the board after those bullies (cowards)
ran past the door:

"You must be the change you wish to see
in the world." —Mahatma Gandhi

And then one more:

"If we cannot end now our differences, at least
we can make the world safe for diversity."
It was John F. Kennedy who said that.

It is Mr. Daly who says:
"And now let us get to work."

Did I mention he's my hero?

Friday, After School

Friday, and I'm meeting the gang
at our favorite place to hang out.
I ask DuShawn to come along,
but he's, like, "Your *gang*."
"Don't say it like that," I say.
"Like what?"

           "Like it's strange."
"Well, why you got to say 'gang'?"
"Why *you* got to say 'got to say'?"
And we go on this way until
"You missed your bus," I tell
DuShawn and there's Tonni's
mother waving and Tonni
shouting, "You want a ride,
DuShawn?" And DuShawn
calling, "Yo, girl, wait up!"
and to me, "See ya, Addie."

           I watch him go
and ask myself, "Now why
is it you love school again?"
It sure is not this part, this
why-do-I-always-say-the-
wrong-thing part, when I don't
even know if I'm saying the
wrong thing.

I pick up my
backpack from where I've
dropped it and call out,
"See ya, DuShawn." But
he's already gone. I hear him
laughing, though.

Thank goodness
for Joe. When I call out "Yo!"
he looks at me like I've grown
another head.

"Dude," he says
as I fall into step beside him,
"you have been spending *way*
too much time with DuShawn."
He decides I'm a "dudette"
and not a "dude," and this gets
me laughing even after I
tell him to stop, and Joe being
Joe, he won't, and that makes
me feel good because it's how
we are, and even when I say
something dumb I never have
to worry I've said something
wrong.

Santa Doesn't Live Here Anymore

We are walking down Main Street in the little town
of Paintbrush Falls, New York, where I have lived
all my life, Joe since the age of four. It's April, and
winter's bite is still in the air, but Santa doesn't live
here anymore. The Easter Bunny in his pastel vest
has taken Plastic Santa's place in the dreary display
window of the Paintbrush Falls Electric & Hardware
Store. "About time," Joe snaps. "Santa must have
been missing Mrs. Claus, and what about the elves
and Rudolph and Blitzer and Madonna and Twister?
Didn't anybody *notice* Santa never made it back
to the North Pole? We should have filed a report
with the Society for the Prevention of Cruelty to
Plastic Santas!" "Are you going to rant like this
the rest of the way?" I ask, and Joe says, "I might.
'Tain't right, Beulah Mae. We got to look out for
our little plastic friends." His rant doesn't end. He
carries on in what he calls his hick-town voice,
punctuating bad grammatical constructions with
Beulah Maes and Jimmy-Bobs, his names for us
in moments like this. I join in, doing my best to
keep up. I know moments like this won't last
forever. One day he'll move away and so will I.
Someone else will have to watch out for our little
plastic friends. Beulah Mae and Jimmy-Bob
won't live here anymore.

Torn Red Leatherette

This is my home away from home,
this booth in the back of the Candy Kitchen,
this torn red leatherette seat,
this place where I meet up with my friends
to talk and to eat.

We call our meet-ups the Forum.
We call ourselves the Gang of Five,
although we were only four at first—
Joe and Bobby and Skeezie and me.
Now we are five or six or even seven,

but it doesn't matter who we are
as much as where we are, and the fact
of the tear in the seat just to the left
of my left hand, the tear I touch
as soon as I sit down, always there.

I never say it, but I think it every time,
how I have been coming here
my whole life, thirteen years. How,
except for the jukebox that's gone,
everything is the same:

The way you can see your face reflected
in the candy case just inside the door.
Across the street, the view of Awkworth & Ames
Department Store. The taste of the shakes.
The size of the fries, long and skinny, like me.

HELLO MY NAME IS, the name tags
read, **CHRIS** or **STEFFI** or **SAM** or **EDDIE**.
"Do you guys know what you want?
I'm ready for your order." And us?
We are always ready.

Skeezie's Fangs

The fries have all been salted and eaten,
except for two Skeezie has tucked between
his lips and canine teeth. "I vant to suck
your blood," he says for the third time.
He has been doing this since third grade,
so no one pays attention except Zachary,
who is new and polite and doesn't know
that to love Skeezie is to ignore him.

"Moving on," I say as Skeezie sucks his fangs
into his maw and his molars move into action,
mashing and grinding and finding more fun
in two sticks of starch than in Disney World
and Six Flags combined. I remind myself
to ignore him and repeat "moving on" when
he belches and says, "Well, excuse *you*, Addie."
Maddening, really, but what can you do?

"This is what I get for hanging out with boys,"
I say with a sigh. "It's an established fact that
boys mature more slowly than girls." The boys—
except Zachary, see above—roll their eyes
as I wonder why it is I *do* hang out with them,
why I am not at the mall with an all-girl posse,
applying lip liner at the Body Shop. Why I am
here, preferring fangs dripping ketchup blood
to lips all glittered and glossy.

The Way the Forum Works

I pick a topic, something really important such as What I'd Do for Love or
    How to End World Hunger,
and then, after we've eaten our burgers and fries (a veggie burger for me,
    on a whole-grain bun)
we order our ice cream and talk about the topic of the day. Well, to be
    honest, it's often about school—
something that happened or something that's going to happen, like an
    election or a dance
or what a teacher had to say or what we think is wrong and needs fixing,
    and that's an endless topic.
I write everything down, every word, even if it's about ice cream or
    Skeezie's french-fried fangs,
because these are the minutes of our meetings and I only wish there could
    be minutes of every minute we live.

Today we discuss the Gay Straight Alliance and the disgusting homophobic
    display put on by the boys
running past room two-twenty-two, the pounding on the door and the
    shouting of names.
We are all very serious, even Skeezie, because he knows enough to know
    that this is about Joe
and Joe is right here at the table. "I think," says Skeezie, "that we should
    track down who did it and
cut off their—" I cut him off, saying, "That's a tad medieval, and one evil
    does not negate another."

Bobby says, "How about the Day of Silence Mr. D suggested?" I write it
down, underlining twice:
<u>a day of no speaking to express solidarity with those who are silenced for</u>
<u>being themselves</u>.

"I don't get it," says Zachary. "Why should anyone have to be silent about
who they are? That's so . . ."
We wait. Is he going to say it? No way. My pencil breaks its point before
Zachary makes his.
He looks at each of us in turn. "That's so ridiculous," he says as the rest of
us exhale collectively.
Joe thinks Zachary is gay but doesn't know it. I agree, but it isn't p.c. to
label, and anyway,
"who cares" is the whole point. It's decided we'll do the Day of Silence,
and I want to talk more
with Joe as we head home together. But Joe's walking with Zachary today
and they're talking video games
and Skeezie says, "I'd like to see *you* be silent for a whole day, Addie!" And
this is the way the Forum works.

Writing it down

is the way I make it real,
the way I find my way
into what it is I feel.

The words on paper or
computer screen
tell me more than
what I knew before
I wrote them,

help me remember
what I'm afraid
I'll forget,

let me keep
what I don't want
to lose,

say to me:
You
were
here.

So I walk home alone

thinking about Joe and how it used to be
before Zachary moved to the neighborhood.
I like Zachary, don't get me wrong, but
I miss Joe when I'm walking home alone.
I think of that poem from the book I read
when I was little, the one that said, "I
loved my friend. He went away from me."

Oh, I know Joe is still my friend and I'm
just being silly, but I miss how we'd talk
and how he'd blurt out "Ministry of Silly
Walks!" and start slicing his legs through
the air like a pair of psychotic scissors,
unhinged and devil-may-care, shouting,
"Keep up, Addie, it's Monty Python Time!"

I could never keep up with Joe, and yet
somehow we'd always end up with our arms
wrapped around each other's waists, kicking
like the Rockettes, or swaying like a couple
of drunks before we even knew what that
meant. Now I walk home thinking the kinds
of serious thoughts Joe helped me to forget.

Grounded

When I get home from school,
there in the front yard my dad
is swinging the three-year-old
from two houses down around
and around. She has one arm
and one leg splayed, reaching
for the sky, her eyes squeezed
tight, her mouth open wide,
crying, "Look at me, I'm flying!"

"Hey, Addie," my dad says as I
say nothing back but run inside
to throw myself on the sofa
and cry. It's ridiculous, I know,
how my body aches to be lifted
and flown. But I will never fly
again. I'm grounded. I'm grown.

Kennedy and Johnson

Cats have radar
for girls who are thirteen
and in tears.
They come out from hiding
or wake from their naps
to rub up against you
or jump in your lap.
And even though they themselves don't cry,
they understand distress.
They never ask why
or what's going on,
they just present themselves
as if to say,
We're here now, you'll be okay.
Kennedy and Johnson
(those are my cats)
are older than me
and wiser, too.
They don't cry
over what's lost
and never again will be.
They don't cry
that they never had a dad
who made them fly

like me.

10 Haikus : 2 Cats

I've known Kennedy
my whole life. "And who are you?"
his eyes sometimes ask.

      He bathes his privates,
      then sweetly comes to kiss me.
      "In your dreams," I say.

The pillow was his.
The sofa he would share, but
the pillow was his.

      Kennedy looked at
      the new cat. He hissed. He spat.
      And then: That was that.

Kennedy's pillow
Kennedy soon discovered
was perfect for two.

      Now they curl in sleep,
      deep in contentment and dreams,
      their heads tucked under.

They demand their food
in the same high voices, then
reject our choices.

Like bookends they sit
on each arm of the sofa,
and we are the books.

Johnson loves to lick.
Kennedy loves to be licked.
Two cats in heaven.

What must it be like
to move through your days always
in step with a friend?

The Girl in the Mirror

The girl in the mirror holds her lifted hand
at the back of her neck, fingering the unseen
clasp to the necklace she has worn every day
since Christmas. She considers her plain face
framed by a drape of straight falling hair: no
drama there, more a face that might be found
on the cover of a novel set on the prairie
than on a poster for a movie about, say,
vampire lust.

Why must she have her mother's face? Her
mother's mother, neither plain nor a beauty,
was always pretty and still is, in an old-
people sort of way. The girl in the mirror
furrows her forehead thinking about her grandmother's arrival the next day. She loves her
grandmother but always feels a little smaller
in her presence. Does her mother feel
that way, too? Does her mother see herself
as ordinary, plain?

My fingers unclasp the necklace. It falls away
into my hand. The girl in the mirror smiles
as we remember the boy who first clicked the
clasp, stepped back to check it out, and said,
"You look nice."

Pretty

My dad tells me I'm pretty,
then laughs and says,
"I guess all dads think
their daughters are pretty."

Thanks, Dad.

Questions I Ask Myself in the Dark

What does Becca Wrightsman want?
Should I let her give me a makeover?
Why would I do that?
Why am I even thinking about it?
Why did Becca have to move back here?
Why did she have to change?
Does everyone have to change?
Does DuShawn like Tonni more than me?
What does he see in me, anyway?
If he breaks up with me,
will I have to give back the necklace?
Why does Ms. Wyman hate me?
Why do I stare at Ms. Watkins' hair?
Why do I notice what she wears?
Will Joe always be my friend?
Does my dad wish I was little again?
Why do I act like I know everything
when inside all I really know are
questions?

Love Songs

The first week of April
and Grandma's in her Birkenstocks

even though we had snow only last week. "Honey," she says, "shoes are foot prisons, trust me. Feet are meant to be free. Now, let me look at you." She's shorter than me by an inch, which is news to both of us. It's only been since the summer that we saw each other and I was looking up at her and she was looking down. The kitchen fixture reflects in her eyes, twin specks of light shining with the intensity of miners' lamps as she turns the beams of her determination this way and that, digging for something, until "Eureka!" she cries. "I hit gold. I see it in your eyes, Addie." "What, Grandma?" "Love, girl!" My face goes red hot as if it were a piece of dry wood her focused rays have ignited. "DuShawn, is that his name? Oh, Lyddie," she says, turning to my mother, who is crushing garlic with the bottom of last year's National Public Radio mug, "how much do you love that our Addie went and got herself a black boyfriend?" "Grandma!" I cry. "I didn't 'go and get' anybody, and it doesn't matter that he's black!" "Exactly my point," she replies, and where have I heard that before. "This is what we fought for, marched for, Lydia, that it wouldn't matter what color anybody's boyfriend is. What about Joe? What's his boyfriend like?" I am tempted to say he's green with orange polka dots, but I tell the truth. "His boyfriend is in the closet, so he doesn't qualify as a boyfriend anymore." "Back in the dark," Grandma says with a click of her tongue. "There is so much work yet to be done." I'm all set to tell her about the GSA, when she takes my hands in hers and says, "I am so happy to be here. I've been lonely."

This is how she is. One minute she's taking on the world and the next she's taking you in her arms. She has been in our house less than an hour. Hugging her, I can't say I tower over her—an inch is only an inch—but for the first time I don't feel small. Maybe this is what it means that I'm growing up. Maybe this is what it means that Grandma is growing old.

With or Without

Grandma has been here for over a week now, sleeping
in the study that doubles as a guest room. She brought her own
coffeemaker because my parents only drink tea, rescued last
year's National Public Radio mug from the garlic, claimed it
as her own. Each morning she sits on the sofa (Kennedy
hunched on the arm behind her looking like a gargoyle, but
fuzzy) with her knees drawn up and her favorite mug, steaming,
held in her hands the way I imagine a priest might hold
the sacramental chalice of wine. As far as I know Grandma
is an agnostic, but she calls the mornings her sacred time.
Maybe she worships coffee. There are people who do. Maybe
she worships a god she doesn't choose to discuss.

On the second day she was here I asked her how long she'd be
staying. "As long as it takes," she said. "You know I'm getting
the house ready to sell. Didn't your mother tell you?" My eyes
welled up with tears. "Oh, Addie, come here," she said. "It's too
much work to keep up that house all by myself, and it holds too
many memories I'd rather keep in my heart, not face every day in
the cupboard where his cereal bowl still sits or there by the side
of his chair in the pile of papers I stupidly refuse to throw out."
"But why do you have to move? I love that house," I said. "I love
it too. But you have to move on. With or without. It's not as if
you have a choice."

Today I had my first cup of coffee. I sat down at the other end
of the sofa, tucking up my knees, cupping the mug the way my

grandma cups my face. Johnson jumped down from his perch behind me, rubbed against my legs, and settled at my feet. I didn't speak, I didn't want to ruin Grandma's sacred time. I thought about my grandpa, gone two years now and his papers still piled by the side of his chair. I looked over at my grandma's face. Her eyes were closed. She was smiling. Maybe she was thinking of him. Maybe she was simply glad that I was there.

Young Man

After they met, Grandma told me, "I like your young man,"
sounding older than she usually does and making me laugh
because, I mean, DuShawn?

              Young man?

                       Not so much.

He did act the part, I guess, asking polite questions
and saying he was sorry to hear her husband had died.
Apparently, I forgot to tell him it was two years ago.
I had this funny moment then, picturing DuShawn and me
together for the rest of our lives and him growing old and
dying the way my grandpa did and what would that be like
and how would I feel.

Lucky is what I felt. Lucky not to be old or sick or lonely.
Lucky to have
          a young man
               my grandmother likes.

Beautiful

DuShawn is the kind of boy
who always has a rubber band
working its way through his fingers,
who thinks spitballs are an art form,
who makes everything into a joke,
including, sometimes,
himself.

DuShawn is the master of sly looks
and cool moves
and smiles that charm the teachers
and, sometimes,
me.

DuShawn never says anything straight
when he can detour to a wisecrack.

But once when it was dark and we were walking and
I told him I'd heard Becca Wrightsman tell Royal Wilkins
I was plain as dirt, he did not take a detour. He said,
"Don't believe what girls say about other girls.
You're beautiful, Addie. They're just jealous."

I didn't say anything then,
and neither did he until
he asked if I wanted a stick of gum.

I said yes, even though I worried
it might be the trick kind
that burns your mouth and
makes you cry.

It wasn't. It didn't.

DuShawn, it seems, is more than
one kind of boy.

Here We Go Again

"Listen to this," I say to DuShawn,
but when he sees I am holding
a book of poems by Langston Hughes,
he says before I can even read him
what I wanted to, "Here you go
again."

"What is that supposed to mean?"
I shoot back, knowing that it means
here *we* go again, that our voices
will start rising and our palms
will start sweating. Let the fighting
begin.

"Why you got to read *that* poet?"
DuShawn asks. "Why you always
Maya Angelou'in' me and askin' me
did I hear that new song by Bee-
Yon-Say? Why you out-blackin' the
black guy?"

"And why are *you* talking like 'you
from the hood,' when the only hood
you've ever been in is the one
on top of your hoodie? Talking
ghetto doesn't make you any
blacker."

"I talk the way I talk, girl," to which
I say, "I am not your girl. I've got a
name." "Yeah?" says DuShawn.
"I got a name for you too, want to hear
it?" I want to throw the book in his
face,

but I like Langston Hughes too much
for that. "I am going in," I tell DuShawn,
and he says, "I'm already gone." He
takes off down the street, leaving me
sitting on my front porch steps alone with
Langston.

I never get to read him the poem.
It isn't about being black.
It's about loving a friend who
went away. DuShawn's friend
Kevin isn't speaking to him
anymore.

I thought he would like the poem.
I thought it might make him feel
better. Well, he probably would have
just snorted and said, "Me and Kevin
didn't love each other, girl. That is
so gay."

Here we go again, throwing words at each other the way people once threw garbage out of kitchen windows, never minding who they might hit in the street below, the empty, stinking bucket still theirs.

I Hate Love

Skeezie bops his head to some song
only he hears (there hasn't been a
jukebox in years), says, "I'm with you
on this one, Addison. Love sucks."

Bobby licks hot fudge from his lower
lip, says you have to work on a
relationship, makes me think he's
been watching too much TV.

Joe reaches for my hand across
the table, says, "It's not like you two
are what you'd call stable. You've
broken up, like, what? Six times?"

"Only five," I mutter, thinking about
our latest fight and how I have no
appetite. I tap the table with my spoon.
My ice cream melts. I don't care.

Hiss and Spit

I'm waiting for Grandma to finish scrubbing the lasagna pan,
my towel at the ready, when one of the cats—Kennedy, I suspect—
hisses loudly in the living room. This is followed by an even
louder hiss, a howl that threatens to become an aria, and
a four-letter word from my dad that he saves for occasions
like this. Grandma laughs and hands me the pan. "Sounds
like your grandpa and me in the early years." "You fought?"
"Oh, honey, he could hiss and I could spit to put those cats
in there to shame. But over time we changed, mellowed
as most people do. Do you and your young man fight?"
"To put those cats in there to shame," I answer. Grandma
laughs again. "Well, I'm not saying it's right, but I'm guessing
it's only wrong if you bring out the claws. That is something
your grandpa and I never did." Later, when the cats are curled
into each other on their pillow and Johnson is licking the top
of Kennedy's head, I see Grandma look up from her book
and nod. "That's right," she murmurs. "That's right."

What We Don't Know

KABUL, Afghanistan – Forced marriages involving girls have been part of the social compacts between tribes and families for centuries. Beating, torture, and trafficking of women remain common and are broadly accepted.

—*The New York Times*

Grandma and I sit reading the *New York Times*,
dusting the pages with powdered sugar from the
jelly doughnuts we have smuggled into the House of
Healthful Eating. We exchange conspiratorial
winks as Grandma says, "What they don't know
won't hurt them."

My mother is out. My father is, in his words,
puttering. I lick powder from my fingers, turn
a page, reach for my mug of coffee, extra light
with lots of sugar. And then I see the photo
of Nadia with her staring eyes and her bandaged
nose. I tell myself not to read the story, but
of course I do.

In Afghanistan there is a girl named Nadia—
only seventeen, not that much older than me—
who had her nose and an ear cut off while she slept.
Her husband was settling a dispute.

Girls as young as six are forced into marriages,
sold for a few hundred dollars to pay off the debts
of their drug-addicted fathers. And their mothers
have no power to change how it goes. They too
have been beaten and raped, sold and traded like
disposable goods, owned by men, while the only thing
they own is their misery, which some trade for
a bottle of rat poison.

The girls at my school talk about makeup and manicures,
clear skin and straight hair, diets and the perfect
nose. Nadia has had six operations and needs more,
just to have a nose through which she can breathe.

And what do I talk about if not clear skin and straight hair?
I talk about Nadia and about Mariam, married at eleven
to a man thirty years older than she, and beaten
for being unable to bear him a child.

I talk about the poems of Naomi Shihab Nye.
I talk about *Sold* by Patricia McCormick.
I talk about suffering and how I don't know
anything about it.

I think I suffer when other girls say cruel things
about me behind my back. I think I suffer when a boy
I like tells me goodbye. I think I suffer when my father
gives me one of his silent looks. But my father

would not sell me for any amount of money. At night
I sleep in a warm bed. In the morning
I sit in a warm kitchen reading the paper,
eating powdered doughnuts.

Nadia says, "I don't know anything about happiness."

I go find my father, give him a hug. "What's up?" he asks.
"Nothing," I say. "Can't a girl just give her father a hug?"
He kisses the top of my head, says, "You smell like sugar,"
and doesn't move until I let him.

The Smell of Clove

Does it count as breaking up if the words are never said?
On Monday DuShawn sidles up to me at my locker, goes,
"What's up, girl?" His fingers working a rubber band, his
jaws chewing gum that smells of clove, the word *girl* full
of honey.

Maybe we half broke up. Maybe when you half break up,
you don't have to say anything. There are so many things
I could say, but I like the smell of clove, and there's his
hand reaching out for mine. "Not much," I say, taking it,
"what's up with you?"

I ♥ Love

At lunch DuShawn says to me,
"You always punctuate my epiphanies
with pain."
                    "Say what?" says
half the table. But I laugh, I get it,
it's our little joke, a line from
one of our two favorite comic strips—
not *Get Fuzzy*, the other one,
about the cow and the boy.

DuShawn gives me his crooked smile,
his face breaking out in dimples,
and I know it's a look that's meant
for only me, and I feel my insides
flip and my brain flop, and I know
I should know better, but so what,
so what.

I heart love.

Old Friends

Another Saturday night and it goes like this:
Bobby's dad calling out, "Anybody home?"
My mom calling back, "Door's open, Mike!"
Bobby poking me, saying hey. We escape
to my room while Mike makes one of his
famous stir-fries and my mom puts her tofu
key lime pie in the fridge to chill.

"Chill," Mike says to my dad, who's asking
what he can do to help. Halfway up the stairs
Bobby and I roll our eyes. Parents
can be *so* embarrassing. Grandma puts out
some cheeses and tells the cats to scat.

Later we all look at old photos Mike found
while cleaning out a drawer. There we are,
Bobby and me, our squishy little faces
almost as red as they are now as we're forced
to look at ourselves as babies. "Always thought
we'd have more," Mike says, and my mother
leaves it unspoken that she and my dad had
always planned to have only one.

The grown-ups get to talking, remembering
this time, remembering that. Slowly the house

fills with love, like a balloon with helium, only
it feels like it's us being filled up, growing light-
headed and silly.

"Life is full of surprises," Mike says, a catch
in his throat. Grandma nods as the palm of her
hand floats down Kennedy's back. "Indeed
it is," she says. They are looking at a wedding
picture of Bobby's parents. Mike asks if he
could have another cup of tea.

Bobby and I have known each other our whole
lives. He's my oldest friend. One day, if we're
lucky, we will be old friends, sitting around
with our kids after supper, looking at photos,
remembering ourselves now, saying life
is full of surprises.

Framed Photo

Bobby's mom was an actress.
I saw her on television once.
Twice, if you count the commercial
for Anthony's Albany Auto.
The main time was when she had a part
on a show I was too young to watch
but my parents let me stay up to see
"just this once" because it was special.
She played a patient in a hospital, dying
of some Hollywood disease.
She looked pale. Her voice sounded soft
and far away. I remember the way she cried
and said, "How can I leave the children?"
I was impressed that she could cry like that.

That night I had a bad dream and crawled into bed
between my mother and my father.
In the morning I wished I hadn't watched,
even if it was exciting knowing that Bobby's mom
was someone almost famous.

A year later she was a real patient
in a real hospital where no one knew
she had once been on TV dying a Hollywood death.
She joked and said, "Too bad I didn't have cancer
before I got that part. I would have been
so much more believable."

Bobby and his dad live in a trailer in Shadow Glen.
A framed photo of his mom hangs on a wall.
The photo is glamorous in a way his mother never was,
but Bobby likes it, and so does his dad,
and so do I because I think it's how
she dreamed herself to sleep at night.
Someone beautiful.
Someone who might be famous one day.
Someone who would grow old
with a scrapbook full of memories.

Her name was Anna Goodspeed.
You probably never heard of her.

Only

It's not like I planned to be an only child.
It's not like I planned to drift to sleep to the sound
of my own voice whispering stories in my own
lonely head. What I planned was a little sister in a bed
just the other side of my narrow room, to whisper back
and giggle and say "It's Addie's fault" when our mom
came to the door and gave us one last warning
to settle down because "tomorrow is a school day."
I would have taken a big brother if a little sister
wasn't available, one who would give me piggyback rides
and teach me knock-knock jokes and say "If those girls
at school bother you again, let me take care of it."

There was a time I had both, a little sister I watched over
and a big brother watching over me. Sometimes all three of us
would sit on the sofa sharing a big bowl of popcorn, even though
if you had walked through the room you would have seen
only me sitting there, my hands passing the bowl back and
forth. You would have heard only my voice laughing
at the parts of the movie we all thought were hysterical.

Maybe this is what it's like for all only children: To love
the family that isn't almost as much as the one that is.

Sweet Dreams

Oh, I don't know if I love DuShawn. I mean,
we're only thirteen. When you come right down to it,
I probably love my cats more, even if DuShawn is the one
who holds my hand and gives me presents and private looks
and never coughs a hairball into my shoe.

But then it'll be late at night and the cats will be off somewhere
doing whatever cats do late at night and my phone will buzz
and it will be a text message saying *sweet dreams*
and I'll text back *you too* and I don't know. Maybe that's love.

Loving Us Our Joni

Grandma is rocking out to Joni Mitchell,
her hips moving slower than the beat and
trying hard to catch up. She winks when
she catches me watching.

"Oh, I do love me my Joni Mitchell," she says.
"Do you love you your Joni Mitchell, Addie?"
"I do love me my Joni Mitchell, Grandma."

Soon we are rocking out together, our hips
catching the beat and riding it like a wave.

The Girl She Was

That's her there,
in the photo with the tear in the corner
and the thumbprint
that can't be wiped away,
wearing shiny white boots up over her knees
and shiny blond hair down past her waist
and a skirt so short you'd think
her mother wouldn't have let her
out of the house.
"Who made you such a prude?" Grandma asked
when I told her that. "I'm still that wild
and crazy girl, Addie, somewhere
behind these drugstore glasses,
somewhere deep inside."

Last summer Grandma took me to a museum
down in Bethel so I could see for myself
what her generation was all about. "Three days
of peace and music" is what they called
the Woodstock Festival. The summer of 1969.
There was a line to get into the museum. "Old hippies
like me," Grandma joked. "But this is nothing.
You should have seen it then. Four hundred
thousand of us. Girls and boys, women and men, and oh
the performers! Joplin and Baez, Country Joe,
Hendrix, Arlo, the Grateful Dead." Grandma shook
her head as we walked past the photos of

the hippies dancing in the mud, the flowers,
the flowing hair, the flashing eyes, the swirling
capes, the sun, and then
the rain
and the rain
and the rain
that never
wanted
to stop.
The gypsy clothes and for some no clothes at all.
I blushed. "Did *you* . . ." I started to ask, and then
it hit me how there was so much I didn't know,
how my grandma was once a girl
who lived in a time I think of as history.
My grandma in her high white boots
and her short short skirt was a mystery I
would never solve, only glimpse in photos and
moments she chose to share.

"I thought it would go on forever," she said,
"that life would always be that good, people
would always be that kind, the music
would never end. How funny to go to a museum
and see your life frozen in time."

That's my grandma, there, with her hair gray
in a braid down her back, dancing to her music,
her Joni, her Joplin, her Country Joe and the Fish,

her bare feet brushing the kitchen floor
as she puts away the dishes.

I wish I'd lived in the Sixties.
I would have made a good hippie, I think,
except I would have kept my clothes on and,
well, those boots were entirely impractical.
But that was my grandma's time and this is mine.
If there is ever a museum about my life, I wonder
what will be in it. What moments will it freeze,
and what will live on, free of photos and memory,
live on in my hair and my hands and my knees
dipping, feet brushing *shush-shush-shush*
across a kitchen floor at twilight.

Love Songs

Grandma and her music, her music, her music, always humming under her breath or listening to her iPod out on her walks or the radio on top of the refrigerator, her CDs, her vinyl, her eyes shut, her eyes open and wet with tears, her feet tapping, her hips swaying, that wisp of a smile.

"What are you listening to?" I'll ask and she'll tell me, "Love songs, honey. All songs are love songs because they're written by people in love with life."

I Think Therefore
I Am Dangerous

I THINK THEREFORE I AM DANGEROUS

"What's that supposed to mean?"
Royal Wilkins asks,
tugging at my backpack,
tugging at my backpack
on the way to gym.
"That button there,
what's it supposed to mean?"
"It *means*," says Tonni,
bumping elbows with Royal
while Becca and some other girls
squeal the Omigod Chorus
somewhere up ahead—
"It *means*," says Tonni,
"that if you think for yourself
you might just *act* for yourself,
you might just shake things up.
Right, Addison?"
"Right, Tondayala," I say,
shrugging my backpack
back on my shoulders,
shrugging my backpack
on the way to gym,
while up ahead, Becca
and some other girls
run their perfectly
manicured fingernails
through their perfectly
straightened hair.

What I Don't Understand About Tonni

Sometimes she acts
like she's my best friend.

Sometimes she acts
like she doesn't know my name.

Sometimes she says,
"Addie, you're so smart!"

Sometimes she says,
"Addie, why you have to all the time act
like you're so damn smart?"

The Omigod Chorus, or What I Have to Listen to Every Single Day

Omigod, did you know?
        Omigod, I hate him so!
Omigod, I love your dress!
        Omigod, your hair's a mess!

Omigod, like like like like . . .
        Omigod, she's such a dyke!
Omigod, he's such a fag!
        Omigod, I love your bag!

Omigod, does this school bite!
        Omigod, I know, right?
Omigod, I need to shop!
        Omigod, I love that top!

Omigod, do I look fat?
        Omigod, what's up with that?
Omigod, I hate my thighs!
        Omigod, I ate those fries!

Omigod, don't be a freak!
        Omigod, that's so last week!
Omigod, is that your phone?
        Omigod, I love its tone!

Omigod, text message me!
Omigod, I hate this tee!
Omigod, I could just die!
Omigod, who's that hot guy?

Omigod, he's kind of punk!
Omigod, he's such a hunk!
Omigod, don't be a slut!
Omigod, keep your mouth shut!

Omigod, you're my best friend!
Omigod, until the end!
Omigod, we are so fun!
Omigod, we're number one!

Devalued

"In what ways do we devalue the English language?"
Mr. Daly asks a class of vacant faces and hidden,
texting hands. I shoot my hand into the air. Mr. D
smiles at me as he moves his eyes across the sullen
seventh-grade landscape. "Does anyone *other* than
Addie have a thought on this? Does anyone *know*
what I mean by 'devalue'?" Now my hand takes on
a life of its own, wagging like an eager puppy. *Me,
me, me*, it whimpers as I try to ignore the snickering
around me.

"Yes, Addie?"

Snickers turn to sighs and groans and cries of *Here
she goes.* "It's when we use empty euphemisms," I begin
(Jimmy Lemon mumbling, "What's a youthanism?"),
"or overuse a word or phrase until it's meaningless."

"An example?"

"'Oh my god,'" I promptly reply, to which Becca replies
under her breath, "Omigod." "Shouldn't that phrase
be saved for religious expression or an occasion
of great emotion? I contend"—here Bobby, my
friend, drops his forehead into his waiting palm—

"that overuse of a word such as 'like' or a phrase such as the one I've just cited, devalues it. Another example is—"

"Thank you, Addie. Let's give someone else a chance, shall we?" Mr. D winks at me as if we're in this together, and I sit down. (Funny, I don't remember standing up.)

Other hands are in the air now as Becca's hand reaches across the aisle and slides a note under my binder. I don't look at it until after class. "You need a makeover in more ways than one," it says.

Now she brushes past, her elbow bumping my shoulder. "Omigod," she says, "so, like, sorry." Other girls giggle, and Jimmy Lemon coughs an insult into his hand. "You're not funny," I tell them, tearing Becca's note neatly down the middle. Bobby waits for me as I gather up my books. He gives me a sympathetic look, one that says he understands what it feels like to be devalued.

Let's Get Addie: Version 2.0

It begins with me opening my big mouth,
which last time I checked was not a sin, but
according to the Gospel of Saint Middle School,
unless you have something dumb to say:
Keep Your Mouth Shut!

So the newest version of Let's Get Addie is in play.
Let's call it Let's Get Addie: Version 2.0, although
believe me when I tell you there have been way
more than two versions. This new version goes
something like this:

Omigod, like, hi, Addie. Addie, like, omigod.
Hey, Addie, like, how's it, omigod, going?
Oh, it's going just *fine*, thank you. I just *love*
listening to your little mouths spout
their little meannesses.

I guess we can't all be geniuses, but can
someone tell me why I should be punished
for having a brain and using it, for opening
my big mouth and speaking a big thought?
Oh my god, I'd really like to know.

Listening from the last stall

in the girls' room on the second floor
I hear Royal Wilkins talking to Sara Jakes.

"Uh-huh, that's what I'm sayin'.
Why we got to sit at the same table,
all cuz she's DuShawn's girlfriend,
and lemme tell you this, girlfriend,
I do not know *how* she got DuShawn
to go out with her, seein' as how
she ain't exactly what you'd call pretty
or cool or nothin'—'cept smart,
I'll give her smart—
but, ew, girl, she got some kind of mouth on her,
always flappin' away havin' somethin' to say,
even Tonni can't keep up with her.
Now why you think DuShawn gone
and fall for a thing like her?
I'll tell you this, uh-huh, DuShawn is her
ticket out of *Un*-popularity, that's right,
and *that* is why she is with him.
But what *he* is doin' with *her*?
Mm-mm, that is anybody's guess."

Sara Jakes uh-huhs and mm-hms
her way along until she asks Royal,
"How's my hair look?"

Royal says, "Pretty as a picture,"
and then adds, "I contend."

They both break out laughing,
not bothering to wonder
who might be in the stall
with the closed door,
and if it might be someone
who often says "I contend"
and never knew two little words
could be quite so

hilarious.

Confession

Sometimes I hide
in the girls' room
on the second floor,
hating myself
for all that I'm not.

But hate is a waste of time

or so my grandma says. "And
that goes for hating yourself
as well as others. Stay soft inside
as the center of a chocolate crème.
Even if your outside is hard,
let it be less bitter than sweet."

The Cure

Some days it really gets to me,
the laughing and mocking, and then
I'll see one of my friends walking
down the hall in my direction, maybe
not even seeing me at first, maybe
busy in his own head, but then
he'll look up and say hey, or smile,

and seeing him gives me back
a part of myself that got lost
for a while. Like today, when Joe
caught me looking mopey and
called out, "Chin up, Beulah Mae!"
It was ridiculous. It was
the perfect thing to say.

TEENAGE GIRLS STAND BY THEIR MAN

the headline reads, and here I stand waving the newspaper
over my head in social studies, trying to get someone
other than Ms. Watkins to hear what I am saying:

"He *hit* her! And then there's this fangirl going, 'I don't think
he'll hit her like that again.' Oh. Really? *Really?* What is *up*
with this fangirl? Is she *excusing* him because he's cute
or hot or whatever it is she thinks he is and she's got his poster
up over her bed and his music bouncing around her head
24/7? Does she think—*does she actually think*—that cute
or hot or whatever they are boys don't hit their girlfriends
again? Or is it because he's a star and stars don't hit,
or at least not more than once?

Hello, fangirl,
he didn't just hit her, he bit her too and nearly choked her.
Did you hear that part, did you think it was a joke?
Do you really mean it when you say, 'She must have made
him mad for him to act that way. If she was dissing him, then
she brought it on.'

Are

you

for

real?"

This is where I take a breath and become aware of Sara Jakes. Her glazed eyes stare at me. Her face, frozen like a death mask, thaws slightly as she slides her tongue over her gloss-slicked lips and prepares to speak. "I think she's right," she says.

"Thank you, Sara."

"Not you, Addie. The fangirl. I mean, why would a big star hit his girlfriend unless she was asking for it? Besides, she forgave him and they're back together. So it's over. And what's it to you, anyway?"

And *this* is the part where I should probably count to ten or simply sit down and shut up, but when I see Ms. Watkins' encouraging look and the sea of nodding heads, most of them belonging to the girls, I can't take it, I have to say:

"Why does it matter to me what some pop star does to his girlfriend? I'll tell you why. I'm a girl too, and I don't want some guy—*any* guy—believing that just because I open my mouth and say what I think that I'm asking for strong and crazy hands to be the voice that answers.

        And I want to know why you don't think he'll hit her like that again, why you don't think he shouldn't have hit her like that in the first place, why you don't think everyone should be safe from being hit or bitten or choked. Why

you

don't

think."

And Sara Jakes says nothing
and the bell rings
and everyone heads for the door
and Ms. Watkins looks over the top of her glasses
and nods and says,
"Good for you, Addie,"
and I say, "Thank you,"
and stuff the newspaper
into my backpack
and gather up my books
and wonder why
I even

bother.

Women Who Love Women

"Women who love women,"
Becca says.
"They're made for each other."

"But Ms. Watkins is engaged,"
says Sara.
"And Addie has a boyfriend."

"So what?"
Becca says.
"They're both feminists.

"And anyway,"
says Becca,
"look at Addie. Just look."

"Look at what?"
Sara says.
"What do you mean?"

"She may as well *be* a boy,"
says Becca,
"with that flat chest."

"She did start that gay group,"
Sara says.
"Why would she do that if—"

"She wasn't gay!"
says Becca.
"How's my lipstick?"

"Totally kissable,"
Sara says.
"Oh, but no homo—"

"Omigod,"
says Becca,
"you're one too."

"Omigod,"
Sara says.
"Gross me out."

Both girls laugh
while I remain hidden,
waiting

for the bathroom door
to shut and the laughter
to die away.

I Just Want to Say

Thinking that Ms. Watkins is brilliant
and beautiful and amazing and wanting to be
just like her and loving the way she dresses
and how the heel of her right shoe slips off
when she sits on the edge of her desk and
crosses her right leg over her left
and watching her bounce her right leg
up and down and wondering if it will
make her shoe fall off
doesn't mean
                  that I'm
                        a lesbian.

Another Thing I'm Sick of Hearing

If I started that gay rights group,
I must be gay.

So if I start an animal rights group,
what does that make me?

A giraffe?

When Silence Is Silenced

Unbelievable. Inconceivable.
That Mr. Kiley would say no
to the first effort of the Gay
Straight Alliance. I say:

Defiance! He may tell us we
can't have our Day of Silence
but silence is a form of free
speech, I contend,

and toward that end I will
be silent on that day to say
NO! to our unprincipled
principal's decision.

Am I being too hard on him?
That's what Mr. Daly says.
He tells me to be patient,
one step at a time, there's
always next year.

But why wait? Mr. Kiley says
he worries about disruption,
that teachers won't be able
to teach, students to learn.

But there's already plenty
of disruption: name-calling,
gossip, notes being passed,
words being whispered,

messages being texted under
desks and shot through space
like armed missiles meant
to destroy. And me?

Will I be a target, brought down
for standing up for my beliefs?
I don't know. I just know this:
I will stand up. I will be silent.
I will let my silence speak.

Shine

DuShawn looks down at the ground, snaps
a rubber band, makes some kind of boy-noise
when it hits some pebbles and sends them
flying. He hasn't answered my question:
"Would you like me better if I let things go,
if I didn't stand up for what I think is right?"

"I might," he says when I ask it again, "but then
you wouldn't be you, so who knows? Maybe
you could just, you know, tone it down."

       "Tone it down?"

"Tone it down, turn it down, whatever. So
you want to go somewhere, do something?"

I kick at the pebbles, say okay, and we go, we do,
we talk about other things or don't talk at all,
and the whole time my mind is racing like
a mouse in a wheel, spinning my thoughts
and getting nowhere but worn out.

       Why should I tone it down,
turn it down, whatever? Is this how it is for girls?
It's okay to be smart until you have a boyfriend,
then you dim your lights so his can shine?

                              Or
is this not a girl/boy thing? Joe told me that Colin
said the same to him, back when they were through
being boyfriends because Colin couldn't cope
with Joe's being so "out there."
                    What's wrong
with being out there, out there like a star
shining in the night when that's the only way
the star can be seen? You never tell a star:

        Hey.
    Tone it down.

It's Just That

DuShawn tells me later,
"It's just that sometimes
you say things in a way
that turns people off,
that makes them not want
to hear you, makes them want
to do anything but listen."

Oh.
It's just

that.

Strong

They say I'm strong,
and I guess I am.

At least I dare
to stand up and speak.

At least I speak
when others do not.

But what is strong?
Is it being brave?

Is it knowing
what you think and feel?

In my beliefs
I am strong as steel,

in my manner
I am strong as rock.

But deep inside
I don't always know.

Does not knowing
mean that I am weak?

Or am I strong
when I do not speak,

but keep silent
and accept the truth:

that I *don't* know,
and that not knowing

is a kind of strength?

So Last Year

"Those shoes have *got* to go," Becca tells me
as if I'd asked, as if she were the Queen of Fashion
and I a lowly peasant scuffing along in straw
slippers. "They are so last year, Addie, so *not*
what everyone is wearing." Do I care?

Later I see this year's shoes staring at me
from the window of Awkworth & Ames, making
their claim on me, shouting, LOOK! HOW COOL!
And I feel foolish for stopping and staring back,
wondering, Do I want a pair?

I never thought about these things before—
clothes, I mean, the shoes that are in, the shoes
that are out—but something about Ms. Watkins
and the way Becca's words are stuck in my head
make me question what I wear.

I don't even like those shoes. I think they're
ugly, if you want to know. "Ugly as sin," as my
grandpa used to say. I wouldn't wear them
if they were giving them away. So why do I
continue to stare?

If I had the right

shoes, if I had the right
shirt, if I had the right
bag, if I had the right
hair, if I had the right
hands, if I had the right
eyes, if I had the right
nose, if I had the right
body, if I had the right
walk, if I had the right
talk, if I had the right
phone, if I had the right
friends, if I had the right
everything, how would
I be different from who
I already am?

It's Like That Old Julia Roberts Movie

The one where Richard Gere takes her shopping in Beverly Hills
on that street where all the stores look like they're temples of satin
and gold and she finds true happiness through clothes. I only know
this movie because Joe has a thing for Julia Roberts and we once
sneaked watching it even though it's R-rated and Joe's parents have
rules about such things. Well, okay,

maybe it's not exactly like that.
I'm no Julia Roberts and my grandmother doesn't look a bit like
Richard Gere and, believe me, there isn't a street within a hundred-mile
radius of Paintbrush Falls like that one in Beverly Hills. But here
we are, the two of us out at the mall on a Saturday, with Grandma
urging me to get whatever I want, it's her goodbye present to me
because she's leaving soon and she says my wardrobe needs serious
help. It's not that I have a bad sense of style, she says, it's that
I have *no* sense of style and if I leave it up to my mother I'll end up
looking more upholstered than clothed.

Grandma loves clothes, but not in the way the girls at school do.
Grandma wears clothes as if she's in a play, and not always playing
the same part. "This is my Rosalita skirt," she'll say, twirling a whirl
of rhinestones and roses. "My Peggy Sue pumps. My Carmen shawl.
Today I am so Mustang Sally."

"Try it on," she insists when I resist an outfit that has "me" written
nowhere near it. "So it isn't you, or at least not the you that you
thought you knew. Put it on and see who you *become*."

I do.

And this outfit that was so not me? Well, it isn't any more "me" when it's on, but it's opened my eyes to the way Grandma sees, opened a door to the possibility that clothes might just be fun.

We shop all day, not just at the mall but at the thrift stores too, the ones down near the bus station and the diner called Betty & Pauls, where they never learned about apostrophes but know a thing or two about how to make the perfect milk shake, and Grandma tells me all the ideas she has for transforming the limp and the lost we've rescued from thrift store hangers and bins into treasures I'll be proud to wear. "Don't think of them as hand-me-downs," she tells me, "but as hand-me-ups!" That's when it hits me how much I'll miss her when she moves back home, and I have to drink the entire rest of my milk shake at one gulp to keep myself from crying.

We make one more stop. "Do you want them?" Grandma asks as we gaze through the window of Awkworth & Ames at The Shoes, enthroned like royalty among the rabble of the other merchandise, looking almost smug. "I kind of hate them," I confess. "I kind of hate that I hate them and want them at the same time. And they're so expensive. I don't know how anybody in this town can afford to buy them. Or why they do." Grandma puts her arm around my waist. "Sometimes," she says, "it just feels good to fit in."

I take one last look at them and shake my head. I can't bring myself
to spend Grandma's money on something I hate. But I don't say no
when she buys me six of the bangles she's noticed that all the girls
are wearing. They're beautiful, and even if it's only my wrist,
it might be nice to have one part of me at least

fit in at last.

Almost Popular

I am almost popular for about three minutes
between first and second period, standing
in front of some lockers in the seventh-grade
hall. Four girls, then five, surround me, tell me,
I love your new look. Where did you get
that skirt? Awesome bracelets. I've got
almost the same ones. We chatter and giggle,
a gaggle of girls, six altogether, did I mention
it was me and five other girls, five popular
girls, our heads together with me
at the center?

It happens in the spring, three minutes
between first and second period,
standing in front of some lockers
in the seventh-grade hall.

Goodwill

By third period the gossip has begun:
Addie buys her clothes from Goodwill.
Even the right bracelets don't count,
it seems, if they're on the wrong wrist.

More Important Matters

I put my mind to more important matters
than what I wear and who notices. I tell myself
it doesn't matter what anyone says. I answer,
"Nothing," when my mother asks, "What's
the matter?" I don't understand these girls,
don't understand what I am to them or why
what I wear or say or do matters. I get tired
of trying to figure it out.

I put my mind to more important matters.

Please Understand My Reasons

PLEASE UNDERSTAND MY REASONS
FOR NOT SPEAKING TODAY.
I AM PARTICIPATING IN THE DAY OF SILENCE,
A NATIONAL YOUTH MOVEMENT
PROTESTING THE SILENCE FACED
BY LESBIAN, GAY, BISEXUAL, AND TRANSGENDER
PEOPLE AND THEIR ALLIES. MY DELIBERATE SILENCE
ECHOES THAT SILENCE, WHICH IS CAUSED BY
HARASSMENT, PREJUDICE, AND DISCRIMINATION.
I BELIEVE THAT ENDING THE SILENCE IS THE FIRST STEP
TOWARD FIGHTING THESE INJUSTICES. THINK ABOUT
THE VOICES YOU ARE NOT HEARING TODAY.

WHAT ARE YOU GOING TO DO TO END THE SILENCE?

"Speaking Card" created by the Gay, Lesbian and Straight Education Network (GLSEN) for the National Day of Silence

Skirmish

Ms. Wyman slaps the card HARD on her desk and snaps,
"Remove that tape from your mouth at once!" almost
knocking the breath out of me. I hold my ground,
shake my head, point to the card, my trembling fingers
telling her: READ!

"Ms. Carrrrrrrlllle," Ms. Wyman purrs. She smiles.
I do not. "Take. Off. That. TAPE!" The class leans
in behind us like we're headline news on CNN:

DEVELOPING STORY!

**ADDISON CARLE, A SEVENTH-GRADE STUDENT IN A SMALL TOWN
IN UPSTATE NEW YORK, SHOWED UP IN HOMEROOM THIS MORNING
WEARING A STRIP OF DUCT TAPE—<u>YES</u>, YOU HEARD THAT RIGHT:
<u>DUCT</u> <u>TAPE</u>—OVER HER MOUTH WHILE HANDING OUT CARDS
STATING HER INTENTION TO REMAIN SILENT ALL DAY IN SUPPORT
OF LESBIAN, GAY, BISEXUAL, AND TRANSGENDER PEOPLE. SHE
IS AT A STANDOFF WITH HER HOMEROOM (AND MATH) TEACHER,
MS. ELLEN WYMAN, WHO IS KNOWN FOR, IN HER OWN WORDS,
"NOT TAKING ANY NONSENSE."**

"I am not in the mood for your rebelliousness, Ms. Carle.
I will not take any nonsense, do you hear?"

I nod, indicating that my hearing is working just fine even if my mouth is immobilized by the strip of silver-gray tape that is beginning to chafe my lips. But I will NOT back down. My eyes let her know this. Her eyes burn in return.

"Fine," she says, "we'll just see what Mr. Kiley has to say, shall we?"

I walk to my seat,
standing tall.
The class cheers.
I bow.
Victory is mine.

For now.

Quack Quack Quack

Ah, the hilarity of the sixth-grade boy who thinks he deserves his own show on Comedy Central just because he goes *quack* when he spots the duct tape across my lips. *Duck tape! Get it? Call my agent!*

The yuck-it-uppers surrounding him slap their thighs and bobble their heads and go *quack quack quack* as I roll my eyes and let it pass.

But of course it doesn't pass. Between every class after that I must endure the contagion of the quacking started by that sixth-grade boy who is undoubtedly basking in his brilliance and planning his career. I bet it

never occurs to him that he really isn't funny. If he had any idea how annoying I find this endless quacking, would he even care? No. He wouldn't even sweat it.

Cacophony

1. harsh discordance of sound; dissonance: *a cacophony of hoots, cackles, and wails*
2. a discordant and meaningless mixture of sounds: *the cacophony produced by city traffic at midday*
—from the Greek: *kakos*, meaning "bad, evil" + *phone*, meaning "voice"

It cannot be a coincidence that Mr. Daly chose *cacophony*
as the vocabulary word of the day. That jangle, that mangle
of language and sound that is the soundtrack of every day
in middle school is even louder to my ears today. It bounces off
my silence like hundreds of thousands of millions of tiny stones
hitting a windowpane behind which I can only watch and pray
the glass will not be broken. I never heard so much until
I spoke so little.

Bad voice, evil voice, multiplied, multiplying, each feeding
on each, reaching my ears with such hateful words, such lies,
such meaningless cackles and quacks, cracks about my sealed lips,
the clothes I'm wearing, the new shoes that are apparently just like
my favorite teacher's. I can do nothing right, it seems.

This babble, this chatter, I tell myself that none of it matters,
that the important thing is to hold my head high and remember
why I am choosing to be silent. I am *not* a lezzie loser know-it-all

big mouth brown-nosing teacher's pet showing off just to get attention. No, whatever their intention, I will let my silence speak louder than their cacophony.

The Silent Ones

There are others who are silent.
I've never noticed them before.
They don't wear tape over their mouths
or look defiant. They look down, or
if their eyes happen to catch yours,
they look away. How many are there
who walk these halls unnoticed each day

while I talk and talk and the loud ones
shout and shove? What do they think of
when they study the floor or glance sideways,
taking a chance that they will not be seen?
What is it they, unseen, are seeing?

That Look

What is that look Ms. Wyman is giving me as we pass
in the hall, the one she wears with such showy
satisfaction? I've seen it before. It's the *I've-just-*
come-from-talking-to-the-principal-and-you're-
in-trouble look. Why so cheery about it, Ms. Wyman?
Why devote so much facial real estate to a gloat?
You hold the power

                but maybe that wasn't always so.
Maybe when you were my age you felt powerless too.
Were you made fun of then as you are now? Maybe
that explains why you try so hard to look so wise.
Maybe that explains the sadness in the corners
of your eyes.

The Other Side

Mr. Kiley sits on the other side of his desk
playing the part of the principal. *Blah blah*,
he is saying, his mouth turned down in self-
importance, or maybe to keep from laughing
at how ridiculous this is. I mean, he's looking
into a face with duct tape where a mouth
ought to be. I hear him ask if I am listening
and I nod and try to look grateful that he's
letting me keep the tape on until lunchtime,
even if after that IT MUST COME OFF!

I notice a photo on the wall behind him.
I don't recognize him at first in that floppy hat
and the T-shirt with a guitar on it and his arms
around two boys on either side of him,
all three of them beaming like they just won
some big prize. The younger boy is missing
two front teeth and the older one holds a fish
on the end of a line.

I'll bet Mr. Kiley is a good granddad.
I'll bet he swivels his chair a lot so he can look
at that photo and see those smiles. I'll bet
he hates having to wear a tie all day and act
like it matters that some girl in his school
is wearing duct tape over her mouth.

I nod when he asks, "Agreed?" and shake
his hand when he extends it and leave
his office thinking I'll never look at Mr. Kiley
in the same way again, now that I've seen
that photo behind his desk and have imagined
him swiveling his chair all day long
just to take another look.

How the Day Is Full of Surprises

The way I can see in ways I have never seen before.
The way I can hear when I'm not busy planning what I have to say.
The way I'm relieved not to be the smart, outspoken one everyone
        expects me to be.
The way it feels good to take a break from the me I expect of myself.
The way none of my friends (except Skeezie) tease me but instead make
        me feel that what I'm doing is real and that it matters.

The way Becca leaves me alone.

The way Ms. Wyman doesn't call on me in math class and allows me not to
        speak.
The way Ms. Watkins admires what I'm doing and likes my outfit and
        doesn't point out that we're wearing the exact same shoes.
The way when the tape comes off, though I remain silent, the scoffing
        and quacking and calling of names begin to fade away.
The way not talking begins to make me feel that I, too, am fading away.
The way a few kids give me a thumbs-up, including some of those who
        are silent most days, who have become visible to me only

Today.

One More Surprise

DuShawn sits at his old table at lunch,
laughing with his old friends,
looks sideways when we pass in the hall,
never reaches for my hand,
keeps his crooked smile and his dimples
to himself.

The first time I speak

Skeezie says, "Ha! I knew you couldn't last the whole day!"
"I was only trying to go to the end of school," I say, the words
feeling strange in my mouth, like food whose taste I'd forgotten.
Shutting my locker, I ask the gang to wait for me before
we head to the Candy Kitchen.

I go to wash my hands. They aren't especially dirty.
Perhaps it's the loneliness I want to wash away.

Taken

The last stall is taken.
I recognize the shoes.

I turn to walk away
but don't get very far

when the stall door opens
and there's Becca Wrightsman,

looking like a rabbit
surprised in the headlights

of an oncoming car.
She doesn't try to hide

eyes that have been crying.
She says to me simply,

"You don't know everything."
And goes to wash her face.

Not Knowing

"Has the cat got your tongue?" Bobby asks.
We are walking and I, uncharacteristically,
am not talking. "You *can* speak now,"
he prods, but all I can give him are uh-huhs
and nods. My mind is on Becca and why
she was crying. It's on DuShawn and why
he was lying when he told me he couldn't
see me later.

       "Wait up!" Joe cries, and he
and Zachary surprise me with hugs from
behind. "Our hero!" Joe says. "We love
your courage, we love your mind!" "We
want to marry it!" says Zachary, though
how they'll marry my mind I really
don't know.

       My mind is full of not knowing,
and if it's true that not knowing is a kind
of strength, then at the rate I am going,
I will soon be the strongest girl
in the world.

Busy

He told me he'd be busy
when I asked him to come over,
there was something about something
that had suddenly come up

and he can't see me all weekend
and I think it's all baloney
or a worse word than baloney
but I don't know about what

and I'm tired of not knowing
but I'll wait it out till Monday
for what*ever* to blow over, then
I might just
           kick
                his
                    butt.

What Was Here

Running in the backyard,
trying to catch a ball and missing it,
I trip on what turns out to be

a two-by-four, the end post
of a swing set long gone.
"Remember, Joe?" I say,

"remember when we were little
and would swing out here
in the summer evenings,

counting fireflies, pumping
higher and higher,
racing to the moon?"

"We never did," says Joe,
as hopeless at throwing balls
as I am at catching them.

What we are doing tossing
a ball around in my backyard
is anybody's guess.

"Of course we did," I insist.
"My mother made us lemonade
and those little butterscotch cookies."

"Nope," says Joe. "I never had
butterscotch cookies, and we never
raced to the moon."

Joe can be so stubborn.
Then I remember:
That old swing set was taken down

the summer I was four,
the summer Joe moved in to
the house next door.

It was someone else I raced
to the moon, a girl who lived
down the street. It was Becca

who loved my mother's
butterscotch cookies,
who counted fireflies,

who pointed her toes to the sky.
It is Becca who would remember
what was here.

Becca

She lived down the street.
Each spring the first tulips on the block
nodded hello from her mother's garden.

When my mother told me she'd moved
to another town, using the word *divorce,*
I nodded in my most grown-up way,

not asking what it meant. I bent
down in their garden later that day,
picked a tulip to take home, peeked

through the window to make sure
they weren't playing a trick, hiding inside
and waiting for me to seek.

The house was empty. The tulips,
all but the one drooping in my hand,
nodded goodbye as I turned away.

Grandma Finds Me

Grandma appears at the back door.
"Stay for supper, Joe?"
"Can't," says Joe, "but thanks."
And off he goes to his house, running
and trying to kick his heels together in the air
and not quite making it and laughing
at himself for not quite making it,
as Grandma lets the screen door
shut softly behind her and comes to me,
pulling her braid over her shoulder
and stroking it like a cat. "I like Joe,"
she says. "I like how comfortable he is
in his own skin."

We stroll around the yard, looking for
tulips. Grandma carries a pair of shears.
I love the word: shears. So old-fashioned
and yet it's what she calls scissors
because it's what her mother called them,
and it's a way for her, she says,
to keep her mother near.

"What were girls like when you were my age?"
I ask as she bends and touches a yellow tulip
the way moments ago she'd touched my arm.
"Did they mess with your head?" I ask. "Did they
act like you were their friend and then talk about you

behind your back? Were there mean girls
when you were my age?"

Grandma's shears go *snip*, and she straightens
herself to look me in the eye. "There have always
been mean girls, Addie. I just don't know
that they were ever so well organized. But then
back in the day we didn't have as many means
of organizing." She leans over and snips. "Cell
phones and the Internet and what have you.
Cruelty has gone multimedia so production
has gone up." She hands me the tulips
and we turn back to the house.

"Rise above it," she says, her hand
on my shoulder. The air is turning colder
as I tell her, "I'll try."

Home

It isn't because I was silent today
and took from the silence lessons to keep.
I have always loved this quiet time of the week,
or have for as long as I've been allowed
to stay up this late. Ten o'clock on Friday night.
Dinner has been eaten, the dishes have been washed
and dried, the cats are curled around somebody's feet.
Kennedy mine, Johnson my mother's. The PBS
documentary on sea turtles ended five minutes ago,
and the TV put to bed. I finger the edge
of my Garfield and Odie bookmark, flip the tassel aside,
find my place in *The Secret Life of Bees*. My father
in his chair is reading too but I can't quite see the title,
and he is already so lost in the words I don't want
to interrupt him to ask. My mother, nestled
in the other corner of the sofa, is knitting another hat
for another child who needs a hat somewhere in the world.

Johnson must be worn out from the day's activities,
whatever they were for him, because he doesn't lift
a paw to bat at the needles flashing and clicking
above his head or the yarn dangling inches from his
whiskers. Kennedy stretches and yawns, looks up at me
with one eye open, one eye closed. I'd tell him he's got
sticky-eye (that's what I call it), but he'd just look at me
as if to say, *Get a life*.

Grandma shakes her head at something she's just read,
takes off her drugstore glasses, and gazes into space.
She'll be going home soon, sitting alone in the living room
she once shared with my grandfather, his chair empty
across from hers, his papers still stacked at its side.
I remember that chair, Grandpa sitting there, me
climbing up his leg and onto his knees when I was little
and he was still strong. How he would bounce me to Boston
to get a loaf of bread. Trot trot home again . . .

Grandma sighs, then winks when she sees me looking.
My mother curses a missed stitch, my father grunts
and turns a page. I roll my head slowly to relieve the crick
that has announced itself in my neck and return to my book
reluctantly, not quite ready to leave Paintbrush Falls, New York,
for Tiburon, South Carolina, to join Lily in her search for a home
when I have found what she is looking for right here.

A Nice Lunch

"I'll make us a nice lunch," Grandma says
the next morning when I find her packing
and go into a pout. "Just you and me.
Your parents will be out. Now, put your
lip back where it belongs." She hands me
a shawl, the one she calls her Carmen
shawl. "Here," she says, "this goes perfectly
with your eyes."

"For keeps?" I ask as if I'm five years old.
"For keeps," she says with a wink. "And I'm just
getting myself organized. I don't leave until next week,
so who knows what other treasures I may yet
bestow upon you. In the meanwhile, how about
I make us a nice lunch?"

How did this happen?
When did my grandmother
become my best friend?

What If

It is not clear what some students at South Hadley High School expected to achieve by subjecting a freshman to the relentless taunting described by a prosecutor and classmates. Certainly not her suicide.

—*The New York Times*

The air is sweet and full of spring
as I read these words, sitting
with my grandmother at either end
of the porch swing, lunch on paper plates
between us, napkins tucked under our thighs
so the wind won't surprise them
and carry them off. They flutter delicately
like scarves.

The girl hanged herself on a bitter winter day,
tired, at fifteen, of the taunts and bullying,
frightened and feeling alone, even though
she had friends and a mother and father
and a little sister who had given her a scarf
for Christmas.

Hours earlier she had cried in the nurse's office.
Walking home, she was hit by a can of Red Bull
thrown from a car by some of the girls who were driven
to hate her, all because she was new to the school,
from another country, had dared to date

one of the popular boys. "Irish slut," they called her.
"Druggie," they called her. Texted her: "You deserve
to die."

Grandma says, "Why are you crying, sweetheart?"
I didn't know I was. I hand her the paper, look out
across the street where some children are playing
hide-and-seek.

What if she had never left Ireland?
What if she had never dated that boy?
What if they had just left her alone?
Why couldn't they just leave   her   alone?
What if her sister had never given her that scarf?
What if her sister had not been the one to find her,
the scarf tight around her neck, her sister
only twelve?
What if her dying means nothing?
What if people just keep on hating?
What if she had been stronger?
What if I were weaker?
What if it were me?

In memory of Phoebe Prince

Ready or Not

"So many bad things can happen," I say.
Grandma gently rocks the porch swing as if we are babies
in a cradle needing to be soothed. "That's true," she says.
"Bad things can happen, and do."

                              "I don't want to know that,"
I tell her. "I'm only thirteen and I've seen too much I don't want
to see." Grandma puts down the paper and reaches for my hand.
"I understand," she says. "Some days I want to put my head
in the sand. There's too much pain out there, there's too much
that scares me. But I wouldn't be able to breathe with my head
in the sand, and I wouldn't be able to see or hear or smell.
The world is a lovely place, Addie, despite the sadness it holds
for each of us, despite the terrible things we do."

I move our plates, scooch close, lean in to her, smell the lavender
of her shampoo. "Maybe it would be better not to think," I say.
"Sometimes thinking hurts."

                         "It isn't the thinking that hurts,"
she says, smoothing my hair. "It's the caring."

We sit quietly for a time, then begin to eat our sandwiches.
The bread is whole wheat, the hummus homemade, the lettuce

crisp and still wet from washing. Across the street, a girl calls out, "Ready or not, here I come."

And I wonder if I am ready, or ever will be, for whatever might come.

We Are Lost
Inside the World

Hey

"Hey," DuShawn says when he sees me Monday morning.
He's acting kind of cool or maybe kind of shy, I can't tell.
"Hey," I say back and want to say something more even if
I don't know yet what it is

                  when Tonni calls his name
like she's calling a dog to come in

                        and DuShawn goes.

Announcement

November 22, 1963:
The day President John F. Kennedy died.
Grandma says she was in history class
when the first announcement
came over the PA:
"The president has been shot."
She was in French
when the second announcement came:
"The president is dead."
Her teacher did not know what to do
so she kept on teaching,
even though tears were streaming
down her cheeks.
Je pleure, vous pleurez, nous pleurons,
tout le monde pleure.
I cry, you cry, we cry,
all the world cries.

On the bus home, some boys made jokes,
but the laughter was forced,
and they cut it out when somebody said,
"Shut up! Don't you get it?
The president is dead!"

For four days the world stopped
as everyone sat in front of their televisions
watching the news unfold in black and white:
the funeral procession,
the pale wife in the black veil,
the little boy saluting his dead father.
Tout le monde a regardé, tout le monde a pleuré.
All the world watched, all the world wept.

Today:
The day my Kennedy died.
I was in math class.
No announcement
came over the PA.
I didn't know until I got home
from school
and my father told me:
"Kennedy was hit by a car
this afternoon. The driver
left a note. She is so sorry.
She didn't see him run out.
She couldn't stop."

The world does not stop today,
there is nothing to see on television,
there is no news about a cat that died
chasing a squirrel on a street
in a little town somewhere.
There is only a little family
and an empty feeling so big
tout le monde devrait pleurer.
All the world should be crying.

bff

I was eight years old when Bobby's mother died,
too young to know what it would be like
to lose your best friend forever.

After the funeral, people came to our house
to eat and talk in quiet voices that grew louder
as the afternoon wore on.
It was summer.

Bobby and I were up in my room
playing Sorry, the Simpsons version,
when it got dark outside the windows
and hushed in the rooms downstairs.
My mom appeared at my door and said,
"Bobby and his dad will sleep here tonight."

Later, I woke up because I needed to pee.
The hall outside my bedroom was dark,
the only sounds a ticking of a clock
and someone crying behind a closed door.
I thought it was Bobby's dad,
or maybe even Bobby.

But it was my mom sitting on the toilet seat
with her head resting on the edge of the sink.
It was my mom who squinted up at me standing
sleepy-eyed in the doorway and said, "Sorry."

Was she sorry for crying
or for sitting on the toilet seat
when I needed to pee?
I didn't ask.

I was eight years old,
too young to know what it would be like
to lose your best friend forever.

A Cat Is Not a Person

Some people say a cat
is not a person.
Those people have never
loved a cat and had one
go and die on them.
You know what those
people know?

Nothing.

Only Johnson

Johnson no longer sleeps on the pillow
he shared with Kennedy.
He has moved to a chair that is more
in shade than sun.
He wakes and looks around
and goes back to sleep
and does not play with any of the toys
in the basket by the door, but sniffs them
and walks away.
Sometimes Johnson jumps onto my lap
and settles in as if to say,
Don't plan on getting up anytime soon.

I have always been an only child.
Johnson is learning to be an only cat.

5 Haikus : 1 Cat

Johnson eats for two—
a cat growing fat from grief,
tasting memories.

Mewing at the door
he waits for it to open,
then waits when it does.

He lifts his butt high,
stretching from toes to tail tip.
Look at me! We do.

Oh, Johnson, I know
what it is to lose someone,
I hear Grandma say.

Johnson sleeps with me,
which he never used to do.
He presses close, purrs.

Tuesday Morning

I do not go to school on Tuesday morning.
My father and mother do not go to work.
Still, the sun comes up and the paper lands
on our front porch and the birds are at
the empty feeder asking to be fed. Grandma
makes extra coffee. Mom makes extra tea.
Dad digs in the far backyard. At noon
we bury Kennedy near the lilac bush where
he liked to hide and surprise the birds.
He never caught any that we know of.
He was too slow or maybe he was just not
all that interested. We bury him
with his favorite toy, which is not really
a toy but an old sock of mine tied with
a long piece of string we called a tail.
We say some words until the words run out
and then we cover him with dirt
and go inside where Kennedy
is not.

How a Cow Pitcher Makes Me Laugh

Bobby and Joe and Skeezie come over in the evening.
I show them where Kennedy is buried and
we tell remember-when stories about him
until it gets dark. Then we all link arms
and go into the house.

Bobby's dad is there and Joe's parents, too.
The grown-ups, drinking coffee, pour milk from
a little pitcher shaped like a cow.
The milk comes out the cow's mouth.
"Oh, great," Skeezie says, "just what I want,
a cow throwing up in my coffee!"
The grown-ups burst into laughter as we—

Skeezie and Joe and Bobby and me—race up the stairs
to my room, where we collapse on the floor and can't stop
laughing for what feels like hours and oh

it feels good

to laugh.

A Pair of Beaded Earrings

Grandma is leaving on Friday,
two days later than planned,
but she can't wait any longer,
the real estate agent is coming
on Saturday to put her house up
for sale. She should move in
with us, I tell her, and she smiles
and says wouldn't that be nice,
but her life is there and she'd
miss her friends.

I'm your friend, I say, and she
smiles again but says nothing,
only hands me a pair of beaded
earrings she made herself
and closes my hand
around them.

A Note

In English class on Wednesday
Becca slides a note under my binder.
"I'm sorry about your cat," it says.
How did she know? I look up
and mouth *thanks.* She smiles
and points back at the note.
"P.S.," it says, "those earrings
are awesome."

Hurt

When DuShawn finally tells me
that he's sorry about Kennedy,
he looks more hurt than I do.
"Why didn't you call me?"
he asks as our hands touch.
And I don't have an answer
as our hands move away.

DuShawn's Way of Making Up

On Thursday DuShawn leaves a comic strip
taped to my locker. He writes, "This is funny
and so are you!" That's his way of saying
let's make up. And so we do.

Grandma leaves me

her coffeemaker,
a book of poetry,
a playlist of her
favorite songs,

sad,
lonely,
not sure
what
I'll do
without
her.

Grandma
leaves.

"It Will Get Better in Time" Isn't a Lie But It Isn't the Whole Truth Either

Days go by.
And nights.
And somehow,
impossibly,
weeks.

Grandma sells
her house, calls,
tells us about
her new
condominium.

I get used to
it being
just me
on one end
of the sofa,

just me,
with Johnson
no longer
perched
behind me

but curled
at my feet

or planted
in my lap,
purring.

I hang out
with the gang
or with
DuShawn,
happy,

but always
knowing
that things
can change,
things
can change.

Tonni Tells All

Tonni grabs me,
jabs me with her words.
"Addie, come with me.
Right. Now."

Tonni pushes me
into the last stall
in the girls' room
on the second floor.

Tonni's eyes are
kind of wild and
full of something
like sorrow.

"Oh, Addie," she says.
"I am so sorry.
So. So. Sorry."
A finger to her lips,

a hand on my shoulder.
Her nails begin to dig.
"Quiet," she whispers,
"someone's there."

We wait for the flush,
the rush of water,
and the footsteps
heading to the door.

Her grip loosens.
Her eyes soften.
And she tells me.
"Today after school."

My eyes ask what.
And she goes, "Omigod,
you don't know.
But everyone knows.

He's breaking up
with you, Addie.
For real this time.
If you need to talk . . .

I'm here for you.
Call me, okay?
Text me. Are you
okay? Hugs."

She leans in
and her arms skitter
around me
like birds
afraid to land.

She leaves me
there in the stall.

Tonni tells all.
Tonni tells nothing.

Just Something We Do

He always says, "Addie, you're too stubborn.
Addie, you push too hard," forgetting
all the times he's too stubborn,
the times he pushes too hard.

I always say, "DuShawn, get serious."
Then he says, "Addie, lighten up."
And I say, "DuShawn, I mean it."
And he says, "You're pretty when you're mad."

We've been going out for seven months,
almost all of seventh grade,
and we've broken up five and a half times.
It's just something we do.

For Christmas he gave me a necklace,
a heart-shaped box of chocolates
for Valentine's Day, and a CD
two weeks late for my birthday.

The CD was more his kind of music
than mine, but I didn't care. I wear
the necklace all the time, and the box
shaped like a heart sits next to my bed.

I grew used to the ups and downs of us,
the breaking up as part of the "us" of us.
So when he breaks up with me today
I don't take it seriously. When he says,

"Addie, I mean it," I say, "DuShawn,
lighten up." But his dark face gets darker
and there's a period in his eyes where
there had always been an ellipsis.

When he walks away without saying
why or what I'd done or hadn't done,
I want to rip the necklace off
and throw it at him. Like in the movies.

But I'm not a drama queen, even
when my heart is breaking. I will keep
the necklace in the heart-shaped box.
The fate of the CD is uncertain.

Drama Queen, Revisited

I throw myself on my bed, sending Johnson flying,
and scream, NO ONE LOVES ME! at the top of my lungs.
My grandmother has sold her house and is moving
into a condominium (a *ridiculous* word), and my cat,
my cat is *dead* (not you, Johnson), and my boyfriend
has broken up with me, and it's all *proof* that no one
loves me or ever will!

And look at me, look at me, what is happening to my body?
NOTHING! I don't even look like a little girl, I look like
a little boy who's been stretched. And yet, and yet, inside
I feel so different, like I don't even know my own body
anymore or trust it to do what it once did on automatic.
It used to be light and airy, like the fairy cape I wore
one Halloween that came all the way from China. Now
it's like an itchy wool coat handed down from a relative
I never even heard of, two sizes too big one day, two sizes
too small the next, weighing me down, tripping me up.

And I want my father to fly me through the air and
I hate it when he treats me like a child, and I want DuShawn
to love me and I don't ever want to speak to him again,
and where is my grandmother when I *need* her, and why
are all my friends boys? And I wish Kennedy was here
(no offense, Johnson) and I wish I hadn't seen DuShawn
go off with Tonni after he broke up with me and I wish
I could see into the future and know that everything

will be okay, even though I'm the kind of person
who can't bring herself to look at the last page of the book
because I don't want to spoil the surprise, but right now
I don't think I can stand the suspense. So tell me, somebody,
tell me everything will be okay, and by everything I mean

me.

Reasons

too tall
too loud
too pushy
too proud

too stubborn
too bright
too outspoken
too white

too bold
too bossy
too fussy
too I told
you so

are any
of these
the reasons
he broke
up with me

I don't know
I don't know
I don't know
I don't know

"We are lost inside the world"

It's a line from a poem by Naomi Shihab Nye
that keeps playing in my head like a sad song
with a familiar melody and words I think
I am beginning to understand.

Addie This &
Addie That

Fun

The girl on the swing calls out,
"Addie! Hey, Addie!"
I can't tell who it is. It's dusk.
It's dark. I'm on my way
home.

She is the only one on the swing set,
the only person in the playground
that I can make out. Who is she
and why is she calling
to me?

It doesn't matter. It's as much
the swing's rise and fall that calls me
as it is the girl's voice. I push open
the iron gate, drop my backpack
by the fence.

"Swing with me, Addie!" Her head's
dropped back, her hair brushes
the ground. Her feet point high
as she pumps and cries,
"To the moon!"

To the moon! To the moon! I know
now who it is, but how can it be?
Why is Becca here, and why
would she want to hang out
with me?

I start to speak, then don't.
I grab hold of the chains,
push back onto the seat,
let go, and begin to pump
my feet.

"To the moon!" I shout as higher
we fly. I know she is there
by the swish of air that sweeps
my side, and the squeak
of the swing,

the steady, reassuring rhythm,
the breathing that breaks into
laughter, the one time she cries
in answer to a question unasked,
"Who cares!"

As it grows dark we slow our
swinging, then stop. Becca drops
her feet to the ground with a gravelly
crunch, says, "That was fun," and
is gone.

I thought that little girls grew up
and never came back. I thought
I knew who Becca was. I pick up
my backpack and say to the night,
"That was fun."

Whatever

The final project of the year.
We'll be working in pairs.
Ms. Watkins calls my name.
Bobby's hand is in the air,
but not before Becca goes,
"I'll work with Addie.
Fine, whatever."

Everyone stares at her.
She shrugs and sighs.

I remember her
calling, "Who cares!"
as she pumped her
swing higher and higher,
and I say, to my surprise,
"Fine with me.
Whatever."

Crooked Smile

Our private language is now extinct.
Our jokes are no longer funny.
DuShawn still has his crooked smile,
but he smiles it just for Tonni.

We meet each other only in glances.
We eat lunch at separate tables.
I see them holding hands each day.
I'll forget him when I'm able.

Spring, When Things Begin to Blossom

One morning, out of nowhere it seems,
there they are, small to be sure, but enough
that I tell my mother it's time for me to get
another bra.

Addie This & Addie That

"Oh my, yes," says the woman who's stopped me
in the lingerie aisle of Awkworth & Ames, me
trying to look like I'm just passing through and not
standing with my mother directly in front of the
junior bras.

"Oh, yes," the woman repeats, "at our house it's Addie
this and Addie that, isn't it, Clay?" The man named Clay
nods and says, "It sure is," even while his eyes are telling us
he's never heard my name before.

"It's so nice to have you back in town," my mother says,
and the conversation is sidetracked into where-
have-you-been and what-have-you-been-up-to and
how-long-have-you-two-been-married, giving me plenty of time
to picture the scene when Becca hears from her mom,
*You'll never guess who I bumped into in the junior bra
department at Awkworth & Ames* and I just know
how that's going to play out at school on Monday so of course
I'm already planning on being sick that day and maybe
all week
              when I realize her mom is speaking to me again:

"I think it's gutsy of you to stand up for what you believe,
wearing that duct tape over your mouth and all. And that time
you told the whole class what you thought about domestic abuse,
or whatever it was, well, Becca says you were just brilliant,

that's all. She only wishes she had your nerve. But I'm sure
she's told you all this herself, she certainly talks about it enough
at home, doesn't she, Clay?" Clay's eyes have strayed to the next aisle
where there's a lot of lingerie involving lace, and I wish I could press
an eject button and be rocketed out of here, but I am riveted
to the spot. How could I not be, when I'm hearing
what I'm hearing?

"That's nice" is all I can think of in response, but it's enough
for Mrs. Wrightsman, or whatever her name is now, to say,
"You should come over sometime, Addie."

"Okay," I mutter as my mother lifts up something involving daisies
and turns to Becca's mom and asks with a laugh, "What *is*
the point of underwire in a junior bra?" And I wonder if there
is such a thing as temporary death, because I have just died
and I can only hope it's temporary.

Butterscotch Cookies

Who knows if she'll remember?
Who knows why I'm doing it?
But when she opens the door,
sees the plate of butterscotch
cookies in my hands and goes,
"Omigod, I haven't had those
cookies in, like, years!" I have
my answer to both questions.

Two Girls, Hanging Out

I can't believe I am sitting
on Becca Wrightsman's bed,
eating butterscotch cookies,
discussing books we've read.

I can't believe she is wearing
a shapeless shirt and jeans
and not an ounce of makeup
and not once acting mean.

I can't believe she is saying
it's been hard for her at school,
trying to fit in again,
trying to be cool.

I can't believe she is crying
when I say I understand,
then telling me she's sorry
for the gossip she began.

I can't believe she is asking
if I still have the board game
we always played at my house,
she can't recall its name.

I can't believe she is laughing
at something I just said.
I can't believe I am sitting
on Becca Wrightsman's bed.

The Funny Thing Is

"On the day you wore that tape," Becca says
just before I leave for home, "things were getting
out of hand, the teasing and the gossiping. I
told my friends I wouldn't do it anymore, and
that's when they cut me out, told me I was a loser
too, told me the same things could happen to
me that were happening to you. That's why I
was crying in the bathroom. I just, well, I guess
I just wanted you to know."

"Thank you," I say. We are standing on her front steps,
waiting for my dad to show up, looking down at our feet
or out at the street. When I spot his car I turn to Becca.
"We have *so* much work to do on this project. Want
to meet tomorrow? My house?"

"Totally," she says. "And, hey, maybe you can find
that game we used to play. Omigod, wouldn't that be
so much fun?"

"Totally," I say. And the funny thing is, I mean it.

When You Least Expect It

Like when you go to put your CD in the player
and Joni Mitchell's in the slot, not because you
put her there but because Grandma left her
behind. Or you call Johnson "Kennedy" for the
third time in one day. Or your hand in the dark
touches the box by your bed and you can't help
yourself, you have to trace its outline with your
fingers and think the word *heart.*

It's those times that surprise you with how much
you can miss a grandmother, a cat, a boy.

Grandma Calls and It's As If She Knows Just What I Need to Hear Her Say

Oh, I know I could have e-mailed,
but I wanted to hear your voice.

No, you keep that CD. Absolutely.
You love Joni as much as I do.

When are you coming for a visit?
The guest room is waiting. I call it

Addie's Room. What? No, I don't
change the name for other people!

Yes, I did see that Op-Ed piece in
the *Times*, and I couldn't agree more.

How's Johnson doing? And how
are *you*, sweet pea? I hope

you're not still moping over that
dreadful boy. No, he *was* nice,

just immature, that's all. I'm
sorry he broke your heart.

When is school done for the year?
Well, you should have a party.

You can *too* dance! Just let the
music carry you, sweetheart.

Remember what I always say:
They're all love songs.

You don't have to have a boyfriend
or a girlfriend to know love.

Just open up your heart and
let the world in. Your heart

is bigger than you can imagine,
and so is the world, and so,

granddaughter, are you.

Letting the World In

It happens so quietly I almost miss it. I am
standing in a doorway with a plate of nachos
in my hands, my dad behind me in the kitchen
calling out, "Don't fill up on those, there are
enchiladas coming!" My mother going, "Oh,
Graham," in a voice that says they have known
each other for a million years. And here,
here, in the living room before me, my friends
are dancing in their funny, awkward way,
Bobby with Kelsey, Zachary with Joe, all trying
to find the beat and not trip over Skeezie's
enormous, outstretched feet.

My own feet begin to move, my knees begin
to dip, my thrift store skirt starts to swirl,
and this is when it happens so quietly I almost
miss it.
                            My heart opens
and the world comes rushing in.

I Am Who I Say I Am

I am who I say I am,
I'm not some fantasy
of how you think you think you know me
or who I ought to be.

I am a girl who is growing up
in my own sweet time,
I am a girl who knows enough
to know this life is mine.

I am this and I am that and
I am everything in-between,
I'm a dreamer, I'm a dancer,
I'm a part-time drama queen.

I'm a worrier, I'm a warrior,
I'm a loner and a friend,
I'm an outspoken defender
of justice to the end.

I'm the girl in the mirror
who likes the girl she sees,
I'm the girl in the gypsy shawl
with music in her knees.

I'm a singer and a scholar,
I'm a girl who has been kissed.
I'm a solver of equations
wearing bangles on my wrist.

I am bigger than I ever knew,
I am stronger than before,
I am every girl I have ever been,
and all that are in store.

I am who I say I am.
I'm not some fantasy.
I am the me I am inside.
I am who

I choose

to be.

Acknowledgments

In one way or another, many voices contributed to the making of this book.

In poetry: Alan Shapiro and my fellow students in Alan's poetry workshop at the Fine Arts Work Center, Provincetown, Massachusetts. In addition to these fine poets, I am indebted to the work of Billy Collins, Donald Hall, Marie Howe, Ted Kooser, Dorianne Laux, W. S. Merwin, Naomi Shihab Nye, Sharon Olds, Mary Oliver, and Linda Pastan.

In song: Leonard Cohen, Ani DiFranco, Thea Gilmore, Patty Griffin, Janis Ian, Joni Mitchell, Tom Waits, Dar Williams, and Lucinda Williams.

In inspiration: Maureen Ryan Griffin, friend and poet, for reigniting my love of poetry. Shari Conradson and her eighth-grade students in Sebastopol, California, for their many letters and insights over the years, with special thanks to Shari for her friendship and to Hannah Maschwitz, who wrote in a letter about *The Misfits*, "I love Addie's character! She's got a strong personality, but sometimes I think that the readers don't actually know what her soft side is." These words were the key that enabled me to open the door to this book after two years of trying.

In Addie-tude: In addition to Shari: Cathryn Berger Kaye, C. J. Bott, Lucy Calkins, Lisa de Mauro, Lisa Duquette, Helise Harrington, Sue Hagadorn, Deborah Holmes, Mary Jane Karger, Connie Kirk, Lisa McGilloway, Jane Roberts, Janet Trumble, and Kate Walton.

In support and friendship: My colleagues, friends, and family. There are too many individuals to mention without fear of leaving someone out, but I must acknowledge my special debt of gratitude to my very supportive family, Sy Bucholz, Dan Darigan, Arielle Ferrell,

Donald Ferrell and Joanna Mintzer, Donald R. Gallo, Robin Jilton, Judy Leipzig and John Gallagher, Tom Owens and Diana Helmer, Richie Partington, Kristy Raffensberger, Richard and Roni Schotter, Ginee Seo, Melissa Whitcraft and Steven Mintz, and Richard Wilson.

In words: John Cavallero, my fellow teachers, and the students in the Coming of Age classes I've taught at the First Unitarian Society of Westchester in Hastings-on-Hudson, New York. The openness with which the seventh- and eighth-graders in these classes talked about their lives had a direct impact on how I thought about Addie's life. Also, the many readers of *The Misfits* and *Totally Joe* who have written to tell me their responses to those books and to share their stories.

In action: Everyone at GLSEN and the many extraordinary educators, parents, and young people who have embraced *The Misfits* and *Totally Joe* and are devoted to ending name-calling, bullying, and homophobia in their schools and communities.

In memory: My parents, Lee Arthur and Lonnelle Howe.

In wisdom and patience: Amy Berkower, my agent and friend of many years; and the folks at Atheneum and Simon & Schuster, including Laura Antonacci, Justin Chanda, Ariel Colletti, Paul Crichton, Michelle Fadlalla, Russell Gordon, Stasia Ward Kehoe, Michelle Montague, Jeannie Ng, Lucille Rettino, Nicole Russo, Elke Villa, Anne Zafian, and especially Namrata Tripathi, my amazing editor, friend, and soul sister to Addie. Her smart, enthusiastic, and delightful company brought joy to the journey.

In everything: My partner, Mark Davis, first reader, wise counsel, and constant sun shining through the clouds of my uncertainty. His advice each morning to have "the best day ever" was easy to follow when each day would be shared with him. And last but never least, my daughter, Zoey, who has informed so much of what I write, how I love, and who I am.

My gratitude to you all.